Praise for
CHRIS CRUTCHER'S
ATHLETIC SHORTS

An ALA Best of the Best Books for Young Adults
An SLJ Best of the Best in Young Adult Literature

"The real theme is growing—grappling with something
tough and finding the courage to carry on.
An involving group of stories. . .thought-provoking."
—*Kirkus Reviews*

"If the stereotype of the 'bonehead jock' is ever to be defeated,
it will be at Crutcher's hands. He and his athlete protagonists
take on such weighty issues as racism. At the same time,
the author makes the world of sports compelling enough to
engage even the most sedentary readers." —*Publishers Weekly*

"Will speak to YAs, touch them deeply, and
introduce them to characters they'll want to know better."
—*School Library Journal* (starred review)

"Mixes poignancy and humor in just the right proportion."
—ALA *Booklist*

ALSO BY CHRIS CRUTCHER

CHRIS CRUTCHER

ATHLETIC SHORTS

SIX SHORT STORIES

A Greenwillow Book

HarperTempest

An Imprint of HarperCollins*Publishers*

"A Brief Moment in the Life of Angus Bethune"
first appeared in Connections, *edited by Donald R. Gallo,*
published in 1989 by Delacorte Press.

Athletic Shorts: Six Short Stories
Copyright © 1989, 1991 by Chris Crutcher

Library of Congress Cataloging-in-Publication Data
Crutcher, Chris.
  Athletic shorts: six short stories / by Chris Crutcher.
    p.   cm.
  "Greenwillow Books."
  Summary: A collection of short stories featuring characters from earlier books by Chris Crutcher.
  ISBN 0-688-10816-4 — ISBN 0-06-050783-7 (pbk.)
  1. Short stories, American. [1. Short stories.] I. Title.
PZ7.C89At 1991   91-4418
[Fic]—dc20   CIP
                                                         AC

❖

First HarperTempest edition, 2002
Visit us on the World Wide Web!
www.harperteen.com

In memory of Gary Deccio
1955–1990
What a wide embrace you had.
We still feel it.

CONTENTS

FOREWORD

In my travels around the country and in letters from readers, I am constantly asked *what happens* to certain characters in my books. Does Willie Weaver make it when he returns to Oakland? Does he come back home to Montana again later? Where does Louie Banks go after graduation? Do Dillon Hemingway and Jennifer Lawless ever get together? Does Jeffrey Hawkins die?

The answer to all those questions is "I haven't the foggiest idea." My stories don't stop because I stop writing them, but my participation in them does. When I come to the last page of any novel, I present the characters to you, the reader. What happens next is up to you.

However, at times I find myself thinking about some of these folks on my own. I have lived the better part of a year with each, have taken long runs, fast motorcycle rides, and cross-country car trips with all of them. So once in a while I check in.

Athletic Shorts provides my avenue to do that— short stories about characters from those books. Some of these stories take place before the time of the book in which the character appeared, some after, but all are enriched, in my mind, by that character's history in fiction.

In my relatively short life as a writer, I have heard my share of praise (for writing about real problems, stories that boys will read, stories that have teaching value and can be used in the classroom), and I have received my share of criticism (for packing too much into one book, for depicting my characters' hardships too graphically, and for using language and ideas that kids don't need to be exposed to). Like most writers, I like to think the praise is well deserved, the criticism harsh and unfair. That allows me to go right on doing what I am doing.

But whether I am praised or criticized, writing is my passion. Whether it be comedy or tragedy or walking that high, thin tightwire between, my passion lies in connecting with people through the written word, through stories. The stories in this collection are stories

I care about. There is a bit of my soul in every one, a bit of the hero that lies within me, a bit of the fool. They are filled with males and females, oldsters and youngsters, gays and straights, blacks, whites, and all colors between. Some are foolish, some heroic; most, in their own way, are both. In other words they are human.

To tell the truth, I like it when my stories are seen by my critics from the same perspective as that in which most human beings are seen by their critics—for doing their best in tough situations, for failure, for excesses, for heart, for the glorious and the ghastly. I hope there is a little bit of all of that in *Athletic Shorts*.

A Brief Moment
in the Life of
Angus Bethune

PREFACE

ANGUS BETHUNE

"A Brief Moment in the Life of Angus Bethune" is the one story in this collection that does not include a character from any of my novels. In the fall of 1988, shortly after finishing writing Chinese Handcuffs and looking for something a little lighter to cool off my word processor, I received a call from Don Gallo, who had previously edited two collections of short stories for young adults. Don asked me to submit a story for his third, to be called Connections, urging me, if possible, to avoid such mainstay subjects of young adult literature as death, disease, and lost love.

When I need a good idea, I run. Something about the cadence of my feet pounding on the road and the rhythm of air flowing in and out of me frees my mind to run to new ideas. It is possible I ran too far that day, or the sun was much hotter than I thought, because when I returned home, I knew two things about my story: It would be about a fat kid with two sets of gay parents (so when he visited his mother, he also visited his step-mother, and when he visited his father, he also visited his stepfather), and his name would be Angus Bethune. I had waited years to use that name.

It was my first attempt at writing a short story, so I felt I had nothing to lose. My ego was not wrapped up in getting it published. What happened next was magical for me. The short-story form forced me to be precise beyond what had been required before, and the process gave me invaluable lessons in word and idea economy.

And I loved the finished product. So much that I wanted to keep it for myself. But I had promised it to Don, and to Don it went.

However, I like to have my cake and eat it. And lick the frosted beaters and sell it at the fair and have people jump out of it. So I took the story back, making it the only story in this collection that has previously appeared in another book.

A BRIEF MOMENT IN THE
LIFE OF ANGUS BETHUNE

Sometimes, when I stand back and take a good look, I think my parents are ambassadors from hell. Two of them, at least, the biological ones, the *big* ones.

Four parents are what I have altogether, not unlike a whole lot of other kids. But quite unlike a whole lot of other kids, there ain't a hetero among 'em. My dad's divorced and remarried, and my mom's divorced and remarried, so my mathematical account of my family suggests simply another confused teenager from a broken home. But my dads aren't married to my moms. They're married to *each other*. Same with my moms.

However, that's not the principal reason I sometimes see my so-called real parents as emissaries from way down under. As a matter of fact, that frightening little off-season trade took place prior to—though not *much* prior to—my birth, so until I began collecting expert feedback from friends at school, somewhere along about fourth grade, I perceived my situation as relatively normal.

No, what really hacks me off is that they didn't conceive me in some high tech fashion that would have allowed them to dip into an alternative gene pool for my physical goodies. See, when people the size of my parents decide to reproduce, they usually dig a pit and crawl down in there together for several days. Really, I'm surprised someone in this family doesn't have a trunk. Or a blowhole. I swear my gestation period was three years and seven months.

You don't survive a genetic history like that unscathed. While farsighted parents of other infants my age were preenrolling their kids four years ahead into elite preschools, my dad was hounding the World Wrestling Federation to hold a spot for me sometime in the early 1990s. I mean, my mom had to go to the husky section of Safeway to buy me Pampers.

I'm a big kid.

And they named me Angus. God, a name like Angus Bethune would tumble *Robert Redford* from a nine and a half to a four, and I ain't no Robert Redford.

"Angus is a cow," I complained to my stepmother,

Bella, the day in first grade I came home from school early for punching the bearer of that sad information in the stomach.

"Your mother must have had a good reason for naming you that," she said.

"For naming me after a cow?"

"You can't go around punching everyone who says that to you," she warned.

"Yes, I can," I said.

"Angus is a cow," I said to my mother when she got home from her job at Westhead Trucking firm. "You guys named me after a cow."

"Your father's uncle was named Angus," she said, stripping off her outer shirt with a loud sigh, then plopping into her easy chair with a beer, wearing nothing but her bra, a bra, I might add, that could well have floated an ejected fighter pilot to safety.

"So my father's uncle was named after a cow, too," I said. "What did *he* think of that?"

"Actually," Mom said, "I think he was kind of proud. Angus was quite a farmer, you know."

"Jesus help me," I said, and went to my room.

As Angus, the fat kid with perverted parents, I've had my share of adjustment problems, though it isn't as bad as it sounds. My parents' gene pool wasn't a *total* sump. Dad's family has all kinds of high-school shot put record holders and hammer throwers and even a gridiron hero or two, and my mom's sister almost made it to the Olympic trials in speed skating, so I was handed a fair-size cache of athletic ability. I am *incredibly* quick for a fat kid, and I have world-class reflexes. It is nearly impossible for the defensive lineman across from me to shake me, such are my anticipatory skills, and when I'm on defense, I need only to lock in on a running back's hips to zero in on the tackle. I cannot be shaken free. Plus you don't have to dig *too* deep in our ancestral remains to find an IQ safely into three digits, so grades come pretty easy to me. But I'd sure be willing to go into the winter trade meetings and swap reflexes, biceps, and brain cells, lock, stock, and barrel, for a little physical beauty.

Which brings me to tonight. I don't want you to think I spend *all* my life bitching about being short-changed in the Tom Cruise department or about having parents a shade to the left of middle on your normal bell-shaped sexual curve; but tonight is a big night, and I don't want the blubbery bogeymen or the phantoms of sexual perversity, who usually pop up to point me out for public mockery, mucking it up for me. I want *normal*. I want *socially acceptable*. See, I was elected Senior Winter Ball King, which means for about one minute I'll be featured gliding across the floor beneath the crimson and gold crepe paper streamers at Lake Michigan High School with Melissa Lefevre, the girl of my dreams—and only my dreams—who was elected Senior Winter Ball Queen. For that minute we'll be out there alone.

Alone with Melissa Lefevre.

Now I don't want to go into the tomfoolery that must have gone on behind the scenes to get me elected to such a highly regarded post because to tell you the truth, I can't even imagine. I mean, it's a joke, I know that. I just don't know whose. It's a hell of a good one, though, because someone had to coax a plurality of more than five hundred seniors to forgo casting their ballots for any of a number of bona fide Adonises to write in the name of a cow. At first I tried to turn it down, but Granddad let me know right quick I'd draw a lot more attention if I made a fuss than if I acted as if I were the logical choice—indeed, the only choice—and went right along. Granddad is the man who taught me to be a dignified fat kid. "Always remember these words, and live by 'em," he said after my third suspension from kindergarten for fighting. "*Screw 'em*.

Anybody doesn't like the way you look, screw 'em."

And that's just what I've done, because my grand-father—on my dad's side—is one righteous dude, and as smart as they come in an extra-large wide-body sport coat. Sometimes I've screwed 'em by punching them in the nose, and sometimes by walking away. And some-times by joining them—you know, laughing at myself. That's the one that works best. But when my temper is quick, it likes to speak first, and often as not someone's lying on the floor in a pool of nose fluids before I remember what a hoot it is to have the names of my mother and father dragged through the mud or my body compared with the Michelin tire man.

So you see, slowly but surely I'm getting all this under control. I don't mind that my detractors—who are legion—will wonder aloud tonight whether it is Melissa or I who is the Winter Ball Queen, a playful ref-erence to my folks' quirky preferences, and I don't mind that I'll likely hear, "Why do they just swim up on the beach like that?" at least three times. What I mind is that during those few seconds when Melissa and I have the floor to ourselves, all those kids, friend and foe, will be watching me *dance*. Now, I've chronicled the major-ity of my maladies here, but none remotely approaches my altogether bankrupt sense of rhythm. When it comes to clapping his hands or stomping his feet to the beat, Angus Bethune is completely, absolutely, and, most of all, irreversibly brain dead.

I've known about the dance for three weeks now. I even know the name of the song, though I don't recognize it, and I went out and spent hard-earned money on dance lessons, dance lessons that sent not one but two petite, anorexic-looking rookie Arthur Murray girls off sharpening their typing skills to apply at Kelly Services. Those girls had some sore pods.

I've been planning for Melissa Lefevre for a long time. I fell in love with her in kindergarten, when she dared a kid named Alex Immergluck to stick his tongue on a car bumper in minus-thirty-five-degree weather for calling her a "big, fat, snot-nosed deadbeat," a term I'm sure now that was diagnostic of his homelife, but that at the time served only to call up Melissa's anger. Being a fat kid, I was interested in all the creative retaliatory methods I could get to store in the old computer for later use, and when I saw the patch of Alex's tongue stuck tight to the bumper as he screamed down the street, holding his bleeding mouth, I knew I was in the company of genius. And such lovely genius it was. God, from kindergarten on, Melissa was that tan, sinewy-legged blond girl with the brown eyes that just make you ache. You ache a lot more when you're a fat kid, though, because you know she was put on the earth, out of your reach, only to make you feel bad. You have no business trying to touch her.

But at the same time my grandfather—a huge silver-haired Rolls-Royce of a grandfather—kept telling me over and over I could have any damn thing I wanted. He told me that down under that sleeping bag of globules I wore beneath my skin beat the heart of a lion and the body of Jack La Lanne. In fact, in the fifth grade Granddad took me down to San Francisco on Jack's sixty-fifth birthday to let me watch him swim to Alcatraz with his hands cuffed behind him, towing a boat on a line with his teeth. He did it, he really did. He still does.

Granddad also took me to San Francisco to see some gay people; but we went to a place called Polk Street, and it didn't help much. I mean, my parents are working folks who are with only the person they're with, and Polk Street was filled with people looking like they were headed for a Tandy leather swap meet. Maybe it helped, though. At least my parents looked more normal to me, although my mother could pass for Bruiser of the Week about fifty-two times in any given year, so *normal* is a relative term.

The bottom line, though, no matter how my grandfather tried to convince me otherwise, was that Melissa Lefevre would remain a Fig Newton of my imagination throughout my school years, and no matter how hard Granddad primed me, I would never have the opportunity for any conversation with Melissa other than one in my head. Until tonight. Tonight I'll *have* to talk to her. If I don't, she'll have only my dancing by which to remember me, which is like Mrs. Fudd remembering Elmer for his hair. It'd be a damn shame.

All I really want is my moment with her. I have no illusions, no thoughts of her being struck blind and asking me to take her home. When you're different, on the down side, you learn to live from one scarce rich moment to the next, no matter the distance between. You become like a camel in a vast scorched desert dotted with precious few oases, storing those cool, watery moments in your hump, assuring survival until you stumble upon the next.

All I want is my moment.

So here I sit, my rented burgundy tux lying across my bed like a dropcloth waiting to be unfolded on the floor of the Sistine Chapel, digging deep into my reserves for the courage not to crumble, hoping for the power to call up the vision of the decent guy I know I am rather than the short-fused, round clown-jock so many people see. What can Melissa be thinking? She'll be there with someone else, of course, so her winter Nightmare on Elm Street will last but a few minutes at most. She's probably telling herself as I sit here that it's like a trip to the dentist. No matter how badly he's going to hurt you, no matter how many bare nerves he drills or how many syringes of Novocain he explodes into the roof of your mouth, in an hour you'll walk out of there. And you'll still be alive.

Of course, Melissa hasn't seen me dance.

My dad was in an hour ago, looking sadly at me sitting here on the side of my bed in my underwear next to this glorious tuxedo, which, once on, will undoubtedly cast me as a giant plum. Dad's the one who escorted me to Roland's Big and Tall to have me fitted, and to make sure I got something that would be comfortable. He's a sensitive guy, one who has always scouted uncharted waters for me in an attempt to clear away at least the huge logs, to render those waters a *little* more navigable.

He wore his Kissbusters T-shirt, with the universal stop sign—a circle with a slash through it—over huge red lips. I gave one to each of my four parents back in junior high when I negotiated the No Kissing Contract. ("I don't care who's with who or what you do in the sack at night," I screamed out of exasperation during one of our bimonthly "absence of malice get-togethers," designed by my parents to cement our extended family solidarity. "Just don't *kiss* in front of me! I'm in junior high now! Look! Under here!" I said, raising my arms, pointing to the budding tufts of hair. "I got a bouquet of flowering pubiscus under each arm! And the jury's in: I like girls! The only people I want to see kissing are boys and girls! Not boys kissing boys. Not girls kissing girls! I want to see boys kissing girls! Understand? Hairy lips on smooth lips! Read mine! Boys . . . kissing . . . girls!" I started to walk out of the room, then whirled. "You know what I need? You ask me that all the time! 'Angus, are you suffering emotional harm because we're different? Angus, are you feeling angst? Angus, do you need help adjusting? Angus, do you want to see a therapist?' I'm not having trouble adjusting! I don't even know what angst is! I don't want to see a therapist! I just don't want to see you *kissing*! You want to know what I need? I'll tell you! Role models! Someone to show me how things are done! Don't you guys ever watch Oprah? Or Donahue?") It was a marvelous tantrum, and effective in that it resulted in the now-famous ironclad No Kissing Contract, which I have since, for my part, dissolved but to which they adhere as if it were the *Kama Sutra* itself. You will not hear the smacking, sucking reverberations of lips parting in passion from lips in either of *my* happy homes.

"The cummerbund is good," Dad says. "It changes your lines, acts almost as a girdle. Don't keep the jacket buttoned for long; unbutton it early in the name of being casual. That way it won't pull tight where you bulge." Dad is the person most responsible for teaching me to dress a body ignored by the sensibilities of the world's clothiers. It was he who taught me to buy pants with a high waist and to go ahead through the embarrassment of giving the salesman my full waist size—instead of cheating a few inches to save face—so I could always get *all* of myself into my pants and leave nothing hanging over. He also drilled into me that it is a mortal sin for a fat man to buy a shirt that tucks in. In short, my father is most responsible for teaching me to dress like a big top.

As he stands staring at the tuxedo, his brain grinding out camouflage intelligence, I read his mind.

"Don't worry, Dad," I say. "I can handle this."

"You've had this girl on your mind a long time," he

says sadly. "I don't want you to be hurt."

I say, "I'm not going to be hurt, Dad," thinking: Please don't make me take care of you, too.

Alexander, my stepdad, walks through the bedroom door, places a hand on Dad's shoulder, and guides him out of the room. He reappears in seconds. "Your father's a pain in the butt sometimes, huh," he says, "worrying about things you wouldn't even think about."

I say, "Yeah, he is. Only this time *I'm* thinking of them. How am I going to get through this night without looking like Moby Melon with a stick in his butt?"

Alexander nods and looks at my near-naked carcass. He is like an arrow, sleek and angular, the antithesis of my father. It is as if minor gods were given exactly enough clay to make two human forms but divided it up in a remedial math class. Alexander is also sensible—though somewhat obscure—where my father is a romantic. "Superman's not brave," he says.

I look up. "What?"

"Superman. He's not brave."

"I'll send him a card."

Alexander smiles. "You don't understand. Superman's not brave. He's smart. He's handsome. He's even decent. But he's not brave."

I look at the tux, spread beside me, waiting. "Alexander, have I ever said it's hard to follow you sometimes?"

"He's indestructible," Alexander says. "You can't be brave when you're indestructible. It's guys like you and me that are brave, Angus. Guys who are different and can be crushed—and know it—but go out there anyway."

I looked at the tux. "I guess he wouldn't wear such an outrageous suit if he knew he looked like a blue and red Oldsmobile in it, would he?"

Alexander put his hand on my shoulder. "The tux looks fine, Angus." He left.

So now I stand at the door to the gym. The temperature is near zero, but I wear no coat because once inside, I want to stay cool as long as possible, to reduce the risk of the dike-bursting perspiration that has become my trademark. No pun intended. Melissa—along with almost everyone, I would guess—is inside, waiting to be crowned Queen of the Winter Ball before suffering the humiliation of being jerked across the dance floor by an escort who should have "GOODYEAR" tattooed the length of both sides. My fear is nearly paralyzing, to tell the truth, but I've faced down this monster before—though, admittedly, he gets more fierce each time—and I'll face him down again. When he beats me, I'm done.

Heads turn as I move through the door. I simulate drying my butt with a towel, hoping for a casual twist-and-shout move. Your king is here. Rejoice. Marsha Stanwick stands behind the ticket table, and I casually hand her mine, eyes straight ahead on the band, walking lightly on the balls of my feet, like Raymond Burr through a field of dog poop sundaes. I pause to let my eyes adjust, hoping to God an empty table will appear, allowing me to drop out of the collective line of sight. Miraculously one does, and I squat, eyes still glued to the band, looking for all the world like the rock and roll critic from the *Trib*. If my fans are watching, they're seeing a man who *cares* about music. I lightly tap my fingers to what I perceive to be the beat, blowing my cover to smithereens. I see Melissa on the dance floor with her boyfriend—a real jerk in my book, Rick Sanford—and my heart bursts against the walls of my chest, like in *Alien*. I order it back. A sophomore server leaves a glass of punch on the table, and I sip it slowly through the next song, after which the lead singer announces that the "royal couple" and their court are due behind the stage curtain in five minutes.

Tributaries of perspiration join at my rib cage to form a raging torrent of sweat rushing toward my shoes as I silently hyperventilate, listening for my grandfather's voice, telling me to screw 'em, telling me once again I can do anything I want. I want my moment.

I rise to head for the stage and look up to see Melissa on her boyfriend's arm, coming toward me through the crowd parting on the dance floor. Sanford wears that cocky look, the one I remember from football, the one he wore continually until the day I wiped it off his face on the sideline during our first full-pad scrimmage. Golden Rick Sanford—Rick Running Back—danced his famous jig around end and turned upfield, thought he could juke me with a couple of cheap high school hip fakes, not realizing that *this* blimp was equipped with tracking radar. It took him almost fifteen seconds to get his wind back. Hacked him off big time, me being so fat and ugly. But now the look is back; we're in his element. He's country club; I'm country, a part of his crowd on the field only.

As they approach, I panic. The king has no clothes. I want to run. What am I doing here? What was I thinking of? Suddenly I'd give up my moment in a heartbeat for the right to disappear. What a fool, even to think . . .

They stand before me. "Angus, my man," Rick slurs,

and I realize it's not a change of underwear he's carrying in that paper bag. "I'm turning this lovely thing over to you for a while. Give her a chance to make a comparison. You know, be a bit more humble."

Melissa drops his arm and smiles. She says, "Hi. Don't pay any attention to him. He's drunk. And even without that, he's rude."

I smile and nod, any words far, far from my throat.

Melissa says, "Why don't we go on up?" and she takes my arm, leaving Rick's to hang limply at his side.

"Yeah," he says, squinting down at the paper sack in his hand, "why don't you go on up? You go right on up behind that curtain with my girl, snowball king."

Melissa drops my arm and grips his elbow. "Shut up," she whispers between her clenched teeth. "I'm warning you, Rick. Shut up."

Rick tears his arm away. "Enjoy yourself," he says to me, ignoring her. "Your campaign cost me a lot of money, probably close to two bucks a pound." He looks me up and down as couples at the nearest tables turn to stare. The heat of humiliation floods up through my collar, and I fear the worst will follow. I fear I'll cry. If I do, Rick's in danger because it's a Bethunian law that rage follows my tears as surely as baby chicks trail after their mama. "Don't you go be puttin' your puffy meat hooks on my girl," he says, and starts to poke me in the chest; but I look at his finger, and he thinks better.

Melissa takes my arm again and says, "Let's go."

We move two steps toward the stage, and Rick says, loud, "Got your rubber gloves, honey?"

I turn, feeling Melissa's urgent tug, pulling me toward the stage.

"What do you mean by that?" I ask quietly, knowing full well what he means by that.

"I wasn't talking to you, bigfoot," Rick says, looking past me to his girl. "I'm asking if my sweetie's got her rubber gloves."

Melissa says, "I hate you, Rick. I really do."

Rick ignores her. "Bigfoot comes from a high-risk home," he says. "Best wear your rubber gloves, honey, in case he has a cut."

In that instant I sweep his feet with mine, and he lands hard on the floor. He moves to get up, but I'm over him, crowding. When he tries to push himself up, I kick his hands out, following his next movements like a cow dog, mirroring him perfectly, trapping him there on the floor. No chaperon is in view, so it isn't totally out of hand yet. When he sees he can't rise, I kneel, sweat pouring off my forehead like rain. Softly, very softly, I say, "You may not like how my parents live. But they've been together since 1971—monogamous as the day is long. That's a low-risk group, Rick. The only person at high risk right now is you."

He looks into my eyes, and he knows I mean it, knows I'm past caring about my embarrassment. "Okay, man," he says, raising his hands in surrender, "just having a little fun."

I'm apologizing to Melissa all the way up the back-stage stairs, but she's not having any. "You should have stomped on his throat," she says, and I involuntarily visualize Alex Immergluck clutching at his bleeding mouth in the freezing cold next to the car bumper. "If you ever get another chance, I'll pay you money."

At the side door to the stage I say, "Speaking of embarrassment, there's something you need to know."

She waits.

"I can't dance."

Melissa smiles. "Not everyone's Nureyev," she says. "We'll survive."

I say, "Yeah, well, not everyone's Quasimodo either. I didn't say I can't dance *well*. I said I can't dance. Good people have been badly hurt trying to dance with me."

We're near the risers on the stage now, and our "court," made up of juniors and sophomores, stands below the spot at the top where we are to be crowned. Melissa hushes me as we receive instructions from the senior class adviser. There will be trumpeting, the crowning by last year's royalty, followed by a slow march down the portable steps to the gym floor to begin the royal dance.

We take our places. The darkness of the stage and the silence are excruciating. "What did he mean, my campaign cost him a lot of money?" I whisper.

"Never mind."

I snort a laugh and say, "I can take it."

"He's rich, and he's rude," she says. "I'm embarrassed I'm with him." She pauses, and slides her arm in mine. "I'm *not* with him. It was supposed to be a lesson for me. . . ."

The curtains part as the trumpets blare.

I gaze out into the spotlights, smiling like a giant "Have a Nice Day" grape. The introduction of last year's king and queen begins, and they move toward us from stage left and right to relinquish their crowns to us. It all would be unbelievably ridiculous even if they weren't crowning King Angus the Fat. Without moving her lips, Melissa says, "I picked a slow song. We don't have to move much. Dance close to me. When you feel me lean, you lean. Whatever you do, don't listen to the music. It'll just mess you up. Trust me. My brother's like you. Just follow."

She grips my arm as the royal march starts and leads me down the risers to the portable steps leading to the dance floor. I have surrendered. If I am to survive this, it will be through the will of Melissa Lefevre.

Somehow I remember to hand her the traditional single long-stemmed red rose, and she takes it in her hand, smiling, then pulls me tight. She says, "Shadow me."

A part of me stays to concentrate, but another part goes to heaven. In my wildest dreams I could never have imagined Melissa Lefevre being *nice* to me in my moment, would never have *dared* imagine holding her tight without feeling pushy and ugly and *way* out of line. She whispers, "Relax," into my ear, and I follow mechanically through a song I'd never heard, not that it would make a difference. When I'm finally relaxed enough and know I'm going to live, the words to "Limelight" filter into my head, and I realize I'm *in* it. Like the songwriter, I fear it yet am drawn to it like a shark to a dangling toe.

"Alan Parsons," she whispers in my ear. "Good lyrics. I love 'em. And I hate 'em. That's what makes a song *good*."

I wouldn't know a good song from a hot rock; I'm

just hoping it's a *long* song. Feeling greedy now, I want my moment to last.

"Angus?"

"Yeah?"

"Do you ever get tired of who you are?"

I pull back a second, but it's like Lois Lane releasing Superman's hand twenty thousand feet in the air. She falls. I pull close again. "Do you know who you're talking to?"

I feel her smile. "Yeah," she says, "I thought so. I know it's not the same, but it's not always so great looking the way I do, either. I pay, too."

She's right. I think it's not the same.

"Want to know something about me?" she asks, and I think: I'd like to know *anything* about you.

I say, "Sure."

"I'm bulemic. Do you know what that is?"

I smile. "I'm a fat kid with faggot parents who's been in therapy on and off for eighteen years," I say. "Yes, I know what that is. It means when you eat too much, you chuck it up so you don't turn out to look like me."

"Close enough for discussion purposes. Don't worry, I'm in therapy for it," she says, noticing my concern. "A *lot* of pretty girls are."

"Actually," I say, "I even tried it once, but when I stuck my finger down my throat, I was still hungry and I almost ate my arm."

Melissa laughs and holds me tighter. "You're the only person I've ever told except for the people in my therapy group; I just wanted you to know things aren't always as they appear. Would you do me a favor?"

"If it doesn't involve more than giving up my life," I say, feeling wonderful because Melissa isn't a goddess anymore and because that doesn't change a thing about the way I feel about her.

"Would you leave with me?"

My foot clomps onto her delicate toe.

"Concentrate," she says. Then: "Would you?"

"You mean leave this dance? Leave this dance with you?"

I feel her nod.

I consider. "At least I don't turn into a pumpkin at midnight. I'm a pumpkin already."

"I like how you stood up for your family. It must be hard. Defending them all the time, I mean."

"Compared to me, a boy named Sue had it made," I say.

The music ends; all dancers stop and clap politely. "I want to dance one more," Melissa says. "A fast one."

"I'll wait over by the table."

"No. I want to dance it with you."

"You don't understand," I say. "When I dance to the beat of rock and roll, decent folks across this great land quake in their boots."

She holds my hand tightly. "Listen. Do what you did when you wouldn't let Rick up. Don't listen to the music; just follow me the way you followed him."

I try to protest; but the band breaks into "Bad Moon Rising," and the dance floor erupts. Melissa pushes me back gently, and out of panic, I zero in, locking on her hips as I would a running back's. I back away as she comes at me, mirroring her every move, top to bottom. She cuts to the sideline, and I meet her, dancing upfield nose to nose. As the band heats up, I remain locked in; though her steps become more and more intricate, she cannot shake me. A crowd gathers, and I'm trapped inside a cheering circle, actually performing the unheard of: I'm Angus Bethune, Fat Man Extraordinaire, dancing in the limelight with Melissa Lefevre, stepping outside the oppressive prison of my body to fly to the beat of Creedence Clearwater Revival.

When the drummer bangs the last beat, the circle erupts in celebration, and I take a long, low bow. Melissa is clapping wildly. She reaches across and wipes a drop of sweat from my brow with her finger. When she touches the finger to her tongue, I tell God he can take me now.

"You bitch!" Rick yells at the door as I help Melissa into her coat. "You bitch! You practiced with this tub of lard! You guys been getting together dancing. You bitch. You set me up." He turns to me. "I oughta take you out, fat boy," he says, but his unimaginative description can't touch my glory.

I put up a finger and wag it side to side in front of his nose. "You know the difference between you and me, Sanford?"

He says, "There's a *lot* of differences between us, lardo. You couldn't count the differences between us."

"That's probably true," I say, closing my fist under his nose. "But the one that matters right now is that I can make *you* ugly."

He stares silently at my fist.

I say, "Don't even think it. Next to dancing, that's my strong suit."

The Pin

PREFACE

THE PIN

In the summer of 1968, when I coached the Spokane swim team, one of my best distance swimmers, Kevin, was a fifteen-year-old boy in constant conflict with his father. He was intelligent, hotheaded, and very funny, struggling to become his own person against an equally willful father who had Kevin's best interests in mind, if not the insight to help his son through troubled times.

Kevin's father approached me on the morning before the day of a long road trip, asking if his son could ride with me to the swim meet because he was afraid he'd kill Kevin if he had to put up with him in the confines of a car for more than fifteen minutes. That afternoon the son made the same request. I had the feeling they were taking each other's measure.

That evening Kevin came to me, near tears, describing

an argument gone sour in which the two had come to blows. As he told the story, he burst into tears.

"Did he hurt you?" I asked.

The tears came harder. "No," he said. "That's the trouble. I think I won."

It's a tough way to pass the torch.

THE PIN

We're eating breakfast. MacArthur is laboring over his Frosted Flakes with a fork because across the kitchen on the floor lies his spoon, a harmlessly spent projectile that only moments ago had Huntley's name on it. MacArthur is almost two. Huntley's one of our cats— and partner to Brinkley. Mac is mangling the cereal; little completes the harrowing ride from bowl to mouth, and as his frustration increases, he stabs viciously at the flakes.

"Mom," I say, "I think my worst fears about Mac are coming true."

"And what are those fears, dear?" she asks, somewhat amused at MacArthur's tenacity.

"That he'll grow up to be a cereal killer."

Mom sighs. "You promised to stop doing that,

Johnny," she reminds me.

"I know. I'm addicted."

"There are places you could go for help. . . ."

"It's better than drugs," I say.

"Not for me, it isn't." She pauses. "You'd better not let your father—"

"I know," I say. "Ten push-ups per word, including the setup. What do you suppose that one would have totaled?"

Mom smiles, dodging the mathematical challenge. Dad would have whipped out his calculator like a six-shooter and spit out my sentence before I could blink.

"Do you think of those just to irritate your father?" she asks.

"No, but that's a great fringe benefit."

My father is the Great Cecil B. Rivers. Three-year three-sport letterman at Coho High School in the mid-1950s and number two wrestler at 177 at the University of Oklahoma after that. Number two is mysteriously absent from his version. Dad and I don't always see eye to eye—to the extent that at times we see eye to black eye. Dad thinks I'm too frivolous to grow up in the world as he knows it, and he's right. I wouldn't want to grow up in the world as he knows it. Dad wants to toughen me up.

Actually things are better now that I'm big enough to make Cecil B. think twice before applying his Mike Tyson disciplinary techniques on me, but I still need to keep an eye on him. I still get even for the old days every once in a while, torment Dad a little when I think he's out of line. Like the time Petey Shropshrire and I injected mink scent into his underarm deodorant. Whew! I don't know how a young stud mink breeds, but it must be through terminally watering eyes, wearing swimmers' nose plugs. We restored meaning to the name Ban that time. Petey sort of likes my dad—almost everyone does—but he told me once if his dad acted like mine acts on a bad day, Petey'd be history. It's not likely he'll ever have to prove that. You get the feeling Petey's dad would shove molten steel slivers beneath his fingernails before he'd lay a hand on that kid.

Actually, from what I see in the newspapers and on TV lately about hardass dudes, my dad's probably only a three or four on a scale of ten. It's just that when he thinks he's not in control of everything, he gets kind of dangerous. I think nobody told him when he decided to have kids—a decision made in a state of severe deprivation, according to family myth—that they'd want to be in control, too. At least over themselves. (The state of deprivation took this form: Mom said, "Cecil, I want to have children," and Dad said, "Well, I don't," and Mom said, "Fine. Then let's make sure we don't do anything that would cause that to happen," and she sat down and waited. Mom was a real fox then. I was born exactly nine months and two hours later. Dad must have agreed to have MacArthur fifteen years later to prove I was a fluke.)

Probably there were some really rocky times when I was younger—though I don't remember them too clearly—because Mom is forever apologizing for letting me go through what she did, and when she's really mad at Dad, she says if she'd had a lick of sense, she'd have left him while he was changing back into his shitkicker boots and jeans between their wedding and the reception. Mom's got some mouth on her. He didn't ever actually beat me or anything like that, but he's always roughed me up pretty good when I don't do what he wants. Either with his open hand on the back of my head or with words. But actually I think her life with him has been worse than mine. At least he still *fights* with me. He's long since quit communicating with Mom at all—which is a lot worse in my book—and my guess is she'll be on the first train out of here the day after MacArthur's high school graduation, in about seventeen long years. He's just a better father than he is a husband, I guess. That's a little like saying I'm a better artist than a ballet dancer. I'm not *much* of either.

Wrestling's my sport, which is another reason Dad and I butt heads. From early November, right after football season, until March, three seconds after my last match at state (where Petey is waiting at mat side with a six-pack of corn dogs and a giant peanut butter milk shake), I'm in a constant state of nutritional deprivation, living on a diet of nuts and leaves and pine sodas (a glass of water with a toothpick). I drop from 185 or so at the end of football, to 160, where I was the runner-up state champ last year and where I intend to be the Man this year. It ain't easy. See, I have to wrestle my mother all the way—who thinks it's criminal to drop a tenth of my body weight so I can roll around in a sweaty heap for nine minutes with another idiot whose mother doesn't have the good sense to make him eat right either—and with my father, who constantly reminds me of his heroics at Oklahoma and calls me a wus every time I come home without my opponent's cauliflower ear in my workout bag. God, Dad can just take the life out of wrestling for me sometimes. Guess I should have known enough to stay away from his sport, though there's something to be said for the fantasy of going one better than he did—of wrestling number one at Oklahoma.

I set the Montana state high school record for the quickest pin during my first match this year—a little more than three seconds—with a lightning takedown that left my opponent aghast at the laws of physics that allowed his body to be so swiftly in motion and then just as swiftly at rest on his shoulder blades. But Dad wanted to know why I didn't string the kid out awhile to give myself some practice. Gimme a break, Cecil B.

I have only a semester of high school left. Part of me wants to wait Dad out, but another part wants to put him in his place so maybe he'll go a little easier on MacArthur. You know, give Dad the experience of humility the Bible says is such a big deal. If I know myself, that second part will win out.

"I think I've found my career," I say at the dinner table. Family Rule 605 says all table conversation will be solemn: talk of world events, school issues, anything informative that the entire family can participate in. Dad's look tells me so far this qualifies. "We had a television screenwriter visit English class today," I continue. "He showed us how to set up a teleplay and told us a little about the kind of money you can make. Then he had us break up into small groups and brainstorm ideas for different kinds of series or newsmagazine programs or whatever."

"That's interesting, dear, but do you think it's something you could seriously get involved in? I mean, television screenwriting—"

Dad waves his hand over the table. "Don't discourage him, Maggie. I think he should explore all possibilities. He's young."

"Yeah," I say. "This was really interesting. In fact, Jenny Blackburn and I came up with an idea he thought might make it."

"Which was?" Dad says.

"We're going to do a situation comedy about a talking horse with an IQ of about forty-three."

Dad's face twitches. He knows . . .

"Yeah," I say. "Gonna call it 'Special Ed.'"

Dad's head bobs like a toy beagle in the back window of a '57 Chevy, calculations whizzing through his computer brain at laser speeds. "That's very funny, John," he says, but he's not laughing. "That's worth exactly one thousand thirty push-ups." Dad has total recall. I've got to learn to cut down on the setup. "I think you're finished with your dinner. Why don't you wait in the living room?"

I stare at my plate, hiding my glee. "Yes, sir."

There is madness to my method. Wrestling is in full swing. I can't eat anyway, and it drives me seriously loony to sit and watch my family packing away steak and potatoes when all I can hope for is that the dishwasher didn't get all the egg off the back of my fork after breakfast. I mean, I'm ready to sit below MacArthur's chair with my tongue hanging out to catch the overflow of strained peas, and Dad simply will not allow me to be absent for our one sit-down *family* meal of the day unless I foul up on protocol. Fortunately my father will tolerate *no* shenanigans at the dinner table. None. "Boys," he says at every opportunity, "eating is not a pretty thing. It is our job as civilized men to learn proper etiquette to make it tolerable." Mom only nods, having long since given up on convincing Dad of anything.

And the push-ups? I'm going to need miraculous strength to win state this year. The cream of the crop at a hundred sixty is a transfer named Butch Lednecky from a little logging town called Trout down in central Idaho. Word has it this guy hires out in the summer as logging machinery. His old man was this legendary eight-man football coach down there before he got the defensive coordinator's job at Montana State.

More often than not, when a guy shows up out of the blue from Podunk High with good numbers and a big rep, he turns out to be a one-move minotaur with a single-digit IQ who self-destructs when he discovers it's a penalty to rip off an opponent's body parts. But it looks like old Butch is for real. He's a natural at a hundred seventy, so he doesn't have as far to drop as I do, and he's tearing up his league. I won't know how I'm doing against opponents he's pureed because it won't be until the end of the season that I'm that light, so the whole thing's a shot in the dark. I feel kind of like Louden Swain from *Vision Quest,* and that makes me proud.

My arms are noodles. I can knock out 100 push-ups every ten minutes while I'm doing homework, then finish up with 100 every five minutes. That's 600 an hour while I'm stuffing my brain; 1,200 when I'm not. I had about forty-five minutes' worth of homework tonight, so you can figure for yourself how long it took to rack off 1,030. Dad critiqued every one. My father considers it a personal sin to fail to follow through with an exacted punishment. If he tells you you're grounded for one week (his shortest grounding on record), you're grounded for a week. If you begin your grounding at high noon on, say, Saturday, and your watch runs a minute faster than his and you let yourself off at eleven fifty-nine on the following Saturday, your grounding starts anew. My dad is a hardass.

One thousand thirty push-ups. My father can count push-ups while he's reading, or watching television, or, for that matter, making love, which I assume is why he and Mom don't do that anymore. (I overheard her talking to my aunt last summer. I guess Dad's never been a real hero in the sack. Once during a fight Mom screamed at him that pushing me around was the *only* way he'd ever prove he was a man. *That* cost me big.) If you try to cheat, you start over. If you lose count, he automatically assumes you're trying to cheat.

A thousand thirty push-ups. My arm bones feel like thousand-watt heating tubes.

I wonder if it's really possible to love and hate somebody at the same time. That's what it feels like with Dad. I hate him because no matter what I do it's never good enough. I hate him because he treats my mother like this robot whose only jobs are to cook his meals and listen to his complaints and his Oklahoma wrestling stories. I hate him when he threatens me. The funny thing is, I don't hate him when he tries to push me around physically, maybe because that's how I think we're finally going to get things settled between us. But I love him, too. I must. I want to show him I *am* good enough. I want to do every one of those 1,030 push-ups to his specs. I want to hand him this year's state wrestling trophy for his den and shake his hand with a grip that will bring him to his knees.

I must be out of my mind.

"Coming to the big game?" Marilyn Waters asks me during first-period English.

"Big game?"

"We're playing volleyball against the parents in two weeks. Wednesday. It's a fund-raiser to send the volleyball team to Southern California for a tournament next July. We thought you could do the play by play over the intercom."

"You want *me* to do the play by play?" I'm excited. Any chance to stand in the spotlight . . . And you should see Marilyn Waters. I'd crawl across three acres of burning hot plates on my hands and knees in nothing but gym shorts to watch her hawk a lugie into a salad bar on videotape. Marilyn Waters is a serious fox. "Yeah," I say, as nonchalantly as possible for a man who wants immediately to mate, "I'll do the play by play. Why me?"

"Because you always tell those awful jokes," she says. "We're getting used to them. While the parents are throwing up, we'll mash 'em into the hardwood."

If Marilyn only realized what a compliment that is. Those jokes are *supposed* to make people sick.

I'm in the center of the circle during workout, taking all comers, when it hits me—and Aaron Phelps lights a friction fire on the mat with my nose as a reward for my distraction. If the volleyball players can play their parents, why can't the wrestlers wrestle theirs? More specifically, why can't I wrestle the Great Cecil B.?

"Rivers! What the hell are you doing?" Coach yells at me from across the mat. I know better than to answer. What the hell I'm doing is messing up.

"Sorry, Coach."

"Tell it to Butch Lednecky," he says.

Coach is right, and I get serious.

"Dad," I say over my main course, a glass of club soda spiced with lime, "how would you like a chance to really teach me a lesson?" Dad has just finished announcing to Mom and Mac and me that from this point on, when we want food passed to us at the dinner table, we must first say the name of the person we want to pass it. That way, he explained, not everyone will have to look around. Though that is not much of a problem among the three of us (it doesn't really include Mac. When he passes food, he *passes* it), I will later thank him when I am eating among large numbers of civilized Americans.

"When will that be, dear?" Mom asks, her eyes rolled back in disbelief.

He leans forward. "That will be at business luncheons, or banquets, or country clubs. Who knows? Don't undermine me, dear."

I resist the urge to say I'll never eat among large numbers of civilized Americans because I'd starve trying to remember all the Miss Manners tidbits he's tried to implant in my brain over the years; I want to stay at the table long enough to issue the challenge. I sip my water, and my seriously deprived tongue cramps around the lime like a fist.

"I welcome any and all opportunities to teach you a lesson, John," he says with some exaggeration.

"Wanna wrestle me?"

He smiles. "What lesson could you learn in a coma?"

He has a point. But I push on. "You're looking a little soft, Dad. You're pushing fifty. The years might be the perfect equalizer."

"I wrestled at *Oklahoma*—"

"Number two at Oklahoma," I correct, hoping to set the bait without losing an appendage before the real match.

"The man who wrestled ahead of me went to the Olympics in his weight division," he reminds me.

"He lost," I remind him back.

Dad puts down his fork. I'm pretty sure my sense of humor came from Mom's side of the family. "You're walking on thin ice, young man," he says. Usually he calls me "young man" immediately before I feel wrenching physical pain.

"There's a way to settle this," I say.

"Name your place."

"High school gym. Two weeks from Wednesday. As a prelim to the parent-student volleyball game."

"You want to be embarrassed in front of your friends?" he asks.

"Better than in front of my enemies."

His steely blue eyes penetrate my skull. "No mercy," he says finally.

"No mercy," I answer.

MacArthur fashions a snowball of mashed potatoes and fires it across the room at Brinkley. I put down my fork and lay a hand on his shoulder. "Mac. Eating is not a pretty thing. It's our job as civilized—"

"That's enough, Johnny," Mom warns.

So I'm wrestling Dad. The instant I know it is the instant I have second and third thoughts. What I haven't said about Dad is that he doesn't weigh two pounds more than he did before his last wrestling match at Oklahoma. He runs seven miles a day, swims three times a week, and lifts weights regularly at his club. The veins on Dad's biceps and forearms look like a detailed street map of Billings.

But he's old. What he hasn't been doing is wrestling, and anyone who wrestles will tell you there's a certain lunatic edge you have to walk, and the only way to stay there is by eating celery sticks and raw spinach and Nutriment and running ten miles a day mummified in Saran Wrap and cranking out daily sit-ups and push-ups well into four digits—preferably in a sauna. Your nose and cheeks should sport permanent mat burns, and if your ears fold inward rather than outward, you're bogus.

Dad ain't been wrestling.

But he wrestled at Oklahoma.
But he wrestled number two.
This may be my chance.

I stand toe to toe with the Great Cecil B. Rivers, one
hand lightly in the crotch of his elbow, the other loosely
at the back of his neck. We are mirror images. Our fore-
heads touch. Coach Everett stands in his starched referee's shirt, arm raised and whistle ready, facing us. Dad
wears his Oklahoma wrestling togs, which fit like the
day he wore them last. For the past two weeks I have
heard him in the wee hours of morning, grunting out
push-ups and sit-ups, and three nights ago I awoke after
midnight to the rapid whap-whap-whap of his jump
rope slapping against his study floor. He hasn't men-
tioned increasing his workouts. In fact, he told me he
was taking a couple of weeks off at the club to even
things out for me. He did nearly match me push-up for
push-up the other night after dinner after I told him I
was writing a novel about our two cats—Huntley and
Brinkley. Huntley is a Manx, a cat with no tail, and
Brinkley is a fast, sleek little gold alley cat. I told Dad I
saw this novel as a classic tale of love and war between
the two protagonists, in which Huntley covets
Brinkley's beautiful tail and is willing to fight to the

death for it. (Dad was already counting words.) In the final scene the two would meet in a dark alley to settle their fate, the prize being Brinkley's beautiful golden tail. Then I told him I meant to call it "A Tail and Two Kitties."

One thousand four hundred thirty push-ups.

I was feeling strong and from the kitchen door told him of my second great novel of the call girl who could command any price because of the size of her luscious breasts. (This one cost me double because Dad didn't think Mac should be exposed to such tawdry tales at the tender age of two, even though I reminded Dad that very recently such things were seen merely as lunch boxes to Mac.) The novel would be called "The Sale of Two—"

"Johnny!" Mom warned, her finger aimed at my chest like a poison blowgun. "Say it and you'll be picking soap shavings out of your teeth till you're thirty."

Dad matched me one for one for the first thousand, then fell off to one for two. I swear, it looks like someone slipped a tennis ball under his skin where his triceps should be. The man's in *steely* shape for a dude pushing fifty.

Coach Everett brings his hand down with the whistle, and my father's hand tightens on my elbow like a

vise. I have to be very careful in close; he has at least fifteen pounds on me.

He dives at my leg for the takedown, but I dance
away a step and fall forward onto his back, twisting
quickly to ride him from behind, hoping to turn him
over with a half nelson; but Dad stands, and I bounce
away to avoid his simply falling backward and turning
me into a pinned grease spot.

He whirls, smiling, his eyebrows dancing.
"Oklahoma," he says.

"Number two," I say back, and go for his leg. I get
the takedown, but his escape is so quick I need a slo-mo
replay to prove I ever had him. The rest of the round is
spent locked in quick takedowns and escapes, each of us
looking for that one opportunity.

When Coach's whistle ends the round, we are
locked in the position in which we started. Dad slaps me
playfully on the side of the head and smiles again.
Playful slaps from my dad make you think you should
answer the phone.

The crowd is evenly split, kids screaming for me,
parents cheering for Dad to win one for the Ancients.
We stand facing each other an instant—Dad staring me
down, daring me to drop my gaze and turn for my
corner—when I see it, behind his eyes, at the corners of

his smile. Dad's tiring, and for a reason I can't explain, a sadness rises in my chest. I turn.

In my corner, I ignore what I saw. Troy Marsh, our mauler at unlimited, and Stephan Stent, a knot of muscle at 103, my self-appointed cornermen for this Generational Wrestlemania, towel me off, dispensing clots of wisdom that could come only from below the neck.

"Time for young sons everywhere to arise," Troy says, "and dig deep furrows in the mats with they daddies' noses." Troy's dad is long gone, having left his mother and four sisters hopelessly mired in the welfare system. He took tonight's coaching assignment like a man with a mission.

"Wear him down a little more," Stephan says. "Stay away as long as you can. Jesus, Johnny, your dad's a *monster*. Doesn't he smoke or anything?"

"Only out the ears," I say.

Troy punches my shoulder. "Well, mess up now, my boy, and your daddy's gonna grab your ankles and make a wish."

Across the mat Coach Everett, the *referee,* for Christ's sake, is giving Dad pointers. I hyperventilate for the rest of my minute, walking down the side of the mat, away from my coaching brain trust, remembering Dad's look.

If I'm not mistaken, there was a trace of desperation.

Coach brings us to the center, and Dad chooses the down position. I kneel beside him, my right arm lightly around his middle, left hand on the crook of his left elbow. Dad will try to step out, and I'll try to drive him down. We both know it. He's told me a million times what a great escape artist he was at Oklahoma. Within a millisecond of the sound of Coach's slap on the mat, Dad is standing facing me, his smile in full bloom. Whatever I saw at the end of the last round is gone, and we're in a death lock. The second round is the first, replayed at fast forward. We're up and down so often I feel like I'm ducking bullets. My strategy becomes survival: Go for the quick takedown and work for a move; get away if it fails, which it does, time after time. At the whistle I'm one point up.

"Pin his ass," Troy says in my corner. He nods across the mat. "Old man looks rode hard and put up wet. Look at 'im."

"You looking at the same guy I am?" I gasp.

Troy grips my shoulders, his playfulness drained away. "He wins, you never live it down," he says through gritted teeth. "This is how you move up. Got to take your daddy down."

It's clear how badly Troy would like that opportunity for himself, to get even with his father for leaving his mom and sisters with nothing but the humiliation of being poor. I wonder briefly how many other kids in the bleachers are rooting for me to make a statement for those of us whose time has come to measure ourselves against our fathers.

I choose the down position, Dad draped over me like a bulldogger. "I'm taking you out," he says. "Tired of messing around. You've looked good in front of your friends long enough."

"That right?" I say, and all our slack pulls tight. This is what I've always hated: the feeling that Dad has to be in control, that when the chips are down, he gets to call the shots, and the rest of us be damned. "Give it your best shot, Oklahoma."

Coach's hand hits the mat like a gunshot, and I lock down on Dad's elbow, rolling hard to pull him over my back to the mat. He must have expected me to step out because he's caught off guard. Suddenly I'm staring down into his astonished face, and his desperation returns. He struggles to throw me off-balance and slide out; but I've got him, and before he can move, I'm winding like a cobra into the guillotine. If I get it, he's done. From a distance it's hard to tell which of us is in trouble. We're both on our backs, wrapped head to toe, but my arm is woven under Dad's neck, around his shoulder, and under his back, where my hands are locked. Dad strains with everything he has left to pull away; but my grip is tight, and I pull hard.

A thousand ringing slaps alongside my head run through my brain, followed by a slide show of Dad belittling Mom, Dad telling us how to eat, Dad telling us when to sleep, when to laugh, never to cry, and I dig deep inside the meanest part of me for the power to force him down. I see him standing over my push-ups, demanding that I address him as "sir," and my muscle is stressed cable. "Get ready, Oklahoma," I grunt. "You're about to feel a land rush on your shoulder blades."

He's locked in a bridge, and I strain harder. The crowd becomes strangely silent—I think it's not sure it wants to see this changing of the guard—and Dad's shoulders inch toward the mat.

"When I get out of this," he grunts back, "I'm gonna hurt you."

Screw you, Dad. And I scream out the punch line of every bad joke I've ever made up or ever heard. "We've come to seize your berry, not to praise it! Bless the beets and the chilled wren!" I yell. "These are the souls that time men's tries! Booty is only shin deep! The beer that made Milfamee walk us! For whom the Tells bowl!" *Screw you, Dad!* and with all my strength I drive back into him. His iron body gives, and I turn up the last bit of tension. A groan rolls out of him, and Coach's hand slaps the mat. I release in exhaustion, and Dad is instantly standing, eyes blazing through me. I reach to shake his hand, a sneer playing on my lip; but he slaps it away, and the cheering and booing and laughing stop. Every man, woman, and child in the gym recognizes this, whether from their nightmares or their daily lives. I'm lost for an instant, confused. "Come on, Dad," I say, offering my hand again. My sneer is gone. "You were good." Again he slaps my hand away and turns, and I reach for his shoulder. Before more than three hundred people my father slaps the side of my face so hard I sit on the mat as if dropped by a hammer.

"Come on, Rivers! Lay off! He's a kid!"

Dad stares into the bleachers, as if slapped back into consciousness himself, and I see his shoulders slump. He gazes back down at me, and I expect for an instant he'll offer me a hand; but suddenly he's walking across the gymnasium floor to the boos of the crowd.

I beat the Great Cecil B. Rivers. So where is my glory?

I didn't stay to call play by play for the volleyball game. My love affair with Marilyn Waters will have to wait. I could no more have remained in that gym and borne my father's shame than fly to the moon.

Mom said, "I'm sorry," when I walked through the back door into the kitchen, and nodded her head toward my father, sitting in the next room in his easy chair, reading a book. I crept silently past him to the stairs.

It's well after one. Someone is moving downstairs. It has to be Dad. God, why did I taunt him? Why couldn't I just win it? *Why couldn't I have lost?*

I stand in the doorway to his study. Dad sits with his back to me in his leather chair, head bent forward. He's paging through something, and I move closer.

"Dad," I say softly, and he starts, swiveling in the chair to face me. Tears have streaked his face. I'd give almost anything not to see this. "I'm sorry. I heard you— You want me to go?"

"No," he says, and motions me toward him.

In his lap, lying open, is my old baby album. Here, decked out in his United States Marine dress blues, he holds me, staring in wonder into my infant eyes. There I perch on an inner tube, a bubble pipe jutting out under his marine cap. Here I'm draped in his Oklahoma letter jacket, sitting high atop a navy fighter jet. Dad watches me look at the pictures.

"I swore it'd be different for you and me," he says.

"What do you mean?"

"That I wouldn't do to you what my dad did to me. Make you feel the way I felt."

"Grampa?"

Dad nods. "Yup. He was good with you, and he's great with Mac. But somehow I guess your own boy gets too close." Tears well up again.

"I'm sorry about the jokes, Dad. I don't know what got into me. If I could take it back, I would. If I—"

"Nope," he says. "This is mine. I've raised you for seventeen years, Johnny. And it's come to this. I wanted it to be different. I really did. I swore . . ." For the first time ever, and I mean *ever,* I hear my father break into sobs. I lay a hand on his shoulder, but he brushes it away.

"You want me to leave, Dad?"

He nods.

At the Winter Sports Awards banquet, my father stands before a crowd of athletes and their parents for the first time since he wrestled me. He is immensely uneasy but determined. Dad is there to re-present the 160 state championship trophy to me. The crowd waits in silence. Dad swallows hard. "I'm going to write a novel," he begins. "An epic novel about our two cats. Their names are Huntley and Brinkley. . . ."

The Other Pin

PREFACE

THE OTHER PIN

There is an idiom in athletics (though when I played sports, people used to say, "There is an idiot in athletics") that humiliation breeds character. As a freshman in high school I was made to go against my two-years-older, fifty-pounds-heavier brother in blocking and tackling drills, in order to experience the character-building adventure of being likened unto a pancake.

My first year as a competitive swimmer in college, my swimming coach entered me in a preseason 200 freestyle race against, among others, Steve Krause, who at the time held the world record in the 1,650 freestyle. Two hundred yards in a traditional twenty-five-yard pool requires one to swim a mere eight laps. When I finished that race, Krause was gone. He wasn't resting comfortably in his lane, shaking hands with the other

competitors; he wasn't even up on the deck drying off.
He was gone.

Petey Shropshrire, small and tentative, is about to
face one of the biggest challenges of his athletic career:
a wrestling match with an athlete all his peers dread to
face. He is plagued by constant, gnawing hunger, as he
is commanded to drop to the lowest weight of his less
than brilliant wrestling career, only to be almost cer-
tainly humiliated at the moment of truth.

The person to whom Petey normally turns for sup-
port—his friend Johnny Rivers—is the person who got
him into this jam in the first place. He finds himself with
no place to turn but the source of the problem itself.

THE OTHER PIN

"I need somebody to wrestle Byers," Coach says, and all the grapplers under 125 pounds stare hard at the mat. Johnny Rivers moves in close to Petey Shropshrire, digging an elbow into his ribs. Petey remains quiet and still as a statue, knowing Coach, like the great moonlight auctioneer he is, will take any sound or movement as a bid.

"Do it," Johnny whispers. "This is a chance to wrestle varsity again. Might get you enough points to letter."

"I'd go with the number one person at that weight," Coach continues, spitting his chaw of tobacco into the paper cup that has been with him so long it seems part of his hand, "but Byers is a special case, and I need a man who can handle that."

No one steps forward.

"*Someone* has to do it," Coach continues. "Chris Byers is gonna be wrestling one-twelve or one-nineteen all year long. Silver Creek has a good team this year; we can't afford to forfeit. An' we ain't gonna. Either I get a volunteer, or I *get* me a volunteer."

"*Do* it!" Johnny whispers again. "It's not gonna be that bad."

"It's humiliating," Petey whispers back. "You don't win against Chris Byers."

"You don't win against Johnny Rivers either," Johnny says. "But that doesn't stop guys from wrestling me."

"That's different. You just win. Byers humiliates."

"That may be. But we've got a good chance to win regionals this year. Maybe even state. *Somebody* has to wrestle Byers. Horseshoe Bend forfeited at that weight and lost the match because of it. We can't afford that, so reach for the sky, sidewinder. Give a little for the cause." Johnny pinches the inside of Petey's leg, hard, and Petey screeches, bolting forward.

"Shropshrire," Coach says. "Gutsy move. I knew a hero would show hisself. A pin'll give you just about what you need for your letter, won't it? You wrestled varsity twice already, ain't you?"

Petey starts to protest the nature of his volunteer

move but knows Coach well enough to know it's a done deal. Petey glances around the room. The other guys at lower weights smile again, all looking tremendously relieved. Petey wonders if this time he has truly bitten off more than he can chew. *Nobody* wants to wrestle Chris Byers. He makes a mental note to launch a pipe bomb through Johnny Rivers's bedroom window tonight. "Yeah, I guess so," he says, but somehow that doesn't ease his sense of dread.

"Look at this as a spiritual challenge," Elmer Shropshrire says. "There's often something to be gained, taking on a task that others shy away from."

"You're not giving me the kind of help I'm asking for, Dad," Petey says. He is again in the familiar spot of having to tell his father what advice he seeks. "You're supposed to say, 'Don't do it, son. You can't win. Save yourself.'"

Elmer sits back. He has dedicated his life to clearing the way for his only child, and he hurts inside each time he fails, which seems far too often. A tall, beefy man with a waistline like an equator and a dearth of athletic talent, he has long been elated at his son's interest in sports. Petey excels at baseball, and that is his love; but in a town as small as Coho, Montana, there are many other opportunities, and for the past two years, mostly because of the urgings of his friend Johnny Rivers, Petey has filled the winter months with wrestling. So far he hasn't been great, but his quickness keeps his shoulders off the mat and his name consistently in the number two spot, with the opportunity to wrestle varsity on occasions when number one wrestles up or down a weight class. Or when it comes time to wrestle the likes of Chris Byers. "What can I do really, son?" Elmer asks now. "What would help you?"

"We could move away," Petey says. "Maybe some other state. After the match we'll have to anyway. I'll be too humiliated to show my face, and unless you and Mom have skin like elephant hide, you'll be too humiliated, too. So just be looking for a new location. Maybe the East Coast. We could get into sailing. Wear those fancy white pants and blue blazers with anchors on the pockets. We'll tell people we're related to the Kennedys. Get a family coat of arms. Cover our tracks, Dad, hear me? Cover them good. No one will ever know I wrestled Chris Byers."

Petey's dad smiles. In truth, it tickles him when Petey gets wound up like this, running 90 mph at the mouth and 10 in the brain. He never teases Petey in this state, however, because Petey takes impending tragedy quite seriously, and laughing at him serves only to aggravate his condition. "Petey," he says when Petey stops to breathe, "you'll do fine. It's only three rounds out of your entire wrestling career, and no matter what happens, it'll be over in ten minutes at most."

"When it's over is when it starts, Dad. Because then I have to shower and dress and face the world. I have to show my face at school, Dad, and on the street. It's Chris Byers this and Chris Byers that all over the sports page after every match. If Johnny Rivers got half that much attention, he'd be all-state without ever stepping on the mat."

"You have to understand it's a human interest story," Elmer says. "No matter how you feel, Chris Byers has gone through a lot, beaten heavy odds. The best thing you can do is go out there, hold your head up, and wrestle your best match. That's all anyone can ask. Anybody wants to give you a hard time after that, that's their problem."

Petey is far from convinced, but nothing can be said to change that. His father's mentality is about as far from that of an athlete as one can get living in a country where the Super Bowl is a national holiday. Petey's abilities remain a total mystery to him, and he can only smile and celebrate that for which he has no feel.

"Jeezus," Johnny Rivers says as he and Petey push through the exit of Cineplex 3 at the Northtown Mall on the outskirts of Silver Creek, "get me away from this popcorn. I swear to God I didn't even see the second half of that worthless flick. My taste buds swelled up so big they blocked my eyesight."

"Me, too," says Petey. "I *hate* when I have to drop weight. From now on I'm telling Coach I only wrestle *up*. Even if it means the rest of my life on JV. If I get any hungrier, my stomach will swell up like a basketball and flies will come to crawl on my eyeballs."

"Man," Johnny says, "no flies better crawl on my eyeballs, I'll pick 'em off and eat 'em. Next year I'm getting on that exchange program to Japan. *Those* guys wrestle with their stomachs. I saw this guy on ESPN last week, his *gut* was bigger than me. Man, think of it. We could be puttin' down ten pounds of burgers right now, for *training*."

"Listen, man, we're way too close to the Food Circus to be talking about this. We need to go in another direction. Where to?"

Johnny's head whips to the right, and he comes to point like the finest of bird dogs. "My God, I'm in lust," he says, ignoring Petey's question and nodding ahead. "Look at that. Just look at that. We don't get to the big city enough. If we had more women like that in our lives, we wouldn't be forced to sublimate our sexual desires rolling around on a Styrofoam mat with stinking, sweaty bodies of our same sex."

"What?"

"Look." He nods again at the two girls ahead no more than twenty-five yards, staring into the window of an exclusive women's clothing store. They talk and laugh easily, and the larger of the two has been cloned from Johnny's Advanced Math Fantasies—necessary daydreams that got him through algebra and geometry in his first two years of high school and that are now saving his life in precalculus. She is tall and dark, with nearly jet black hair, and eyes so green he could mow them.

"I've gotta talk to that girl," he says. "I've gotta. God makes you suffer, Petey. He really does. He calls you mysteriously to the mall to a movie *I* could have written—and I can barely write my name—directs you to the seats nearest in the house to the popcorn machine, *knowing*—because God knows all, right?—

that if you eat, you die at the hands of a subhuman small-town wrestling coach with a gut the size of a small prairie dog community. The fat kid next to you stuffs enough malted milk balls and licorice whips into his mouth to make Willie Wonka blanch, and you want to kill him, but you know if you do, you'll eat his stuff to mark your conquest and weigh in a pound over come Friday night. In other words, God creates for you hell on earth. And just when you're about to pack your stuff and move to western Montana or northern Idaho to join a devil cult just to get even, the Lord our God reveals his plan to you. You are Job, really, and He is about to reward you for your patience, with"—and Johnny points to the strong, dark, leggy beauty in front of them—"her."

"Oh, no, you don't, Johnny Rivers," Petey protests. "You know what happens when I try to talk to girls I don't know. I can't talk to girls I do know. Oh, no, you don't. We go over there, you tell one of those stupid jokes you make up all the time, like 'We do not know For Whom the Tells Bowl,' and embarrass us both so bad we ought to shoot ourselves in the head on the spot, but you're too thickheaded to be embarrassed, so you tell another one. Then you start talking to the girl *you* like, which is the one I'd like, too, if I could untie the knot in my tongue, and I'm stuck with the other one, who would rather be talking to you anyway because I'm a squirrelly geek, which is why I can't talk in the first place."

Johnny shakes his head. "You can't be a winner with that kind of attitude. Look, the girl with her is cute. In fact, she's a fox. We can't lose on this one, Peter, my boy. This is God's plan."

"I don't believe in God anymore," Petey says. "Not after right this minute. For one thing, if God would reveal a plan to Johnny Rivers, there's something wrong with Him, like probably the real God's on vacation and some warped kind of angel who was supposed to go straight to hell but slipped through anyway has snuck into the control room and—"

"No time for biblical theories right now," Johnny says, elbowing him. "They're getting away."

In spite of Petey's continued protests, they follow the girls down the long corridor between small shops and around the corner toward the Northtown Mall Food Circus.

Petey's heels dig in. "This part of God's plan, too?" Petey says in the face of a dozen neon signs flashing the names of a dozen eateries, featuring pizza to tacos to fried chicken to Greek sandwiches on pita bread. Saliva pours onto his tongue like a river. "Johnny, don't do it.

They're going toward the *food*."

"Be calm," Johnny says. "This is a test to prove our love."

"*I'm* not in love," Petey said. "I'm *hungry*. Don't you see, if I spend ten more seconds within a hundred yards of Pizza Hut, I'll kick out their window and eat raw dough. Don't do this to me, Johnny. There is no good to come of this. I'm starving myself to wrestle Chris Byers. *Chris Byers,* Johnny. Chris Byers, who, along with everything else, is strong as a bull. Chris Byers has to *gain* weight to wrestle one-nineteen. While my taste buds are cannibalizing *each other* to stay alive, Chris Byers is probably locked *inside* a Burger King somewhere, trying to make weight. I came to the movies with you today to try to forget my pain, Johnny, not double it. I'm giving you one chance to save our friendship. Don't follow those girls into the food section of this mall. I'm drawing the line here, Rivers. Don't take one more step."

"I'm doing this for you, Petey," Johnny says, shaking his head again and locking his fingers around Petey's elbow. "This is the kind of challenge that spiritually prepares you to take on a wrestler with the unique capabilities of Chris Byers. I'm as hungry as you are, and I can take it."

"Yeah, but you're after something a lot more spiritual than food."

Johnny stops, Petey's elbow still locked in his grip, and stares through the window of Taco Tango, where his eyes meet the gaze of the girl of his dreams. In a final, futile effort, Petey says, "Don't do this," but there is nothing left of his resolve.

At the counter Johnny orders an extra large Taco Tango Mango Shake with three cups. Petey's tongue cramps into a tube, and spittle runs off his chin like a high African waterfall. "What are you *doing*? Get that thing away from me. I swear, I'll knock it over. I will."

"They won't let us sit here if we don't order. Relax, Pete. Sometimes there are dues to pay."

Petey's voice rises to that preadolescent pitch it always hits when he feels his life spinning out of control. "Dues are what Boy Scouts pay," he eeps. "My mom and dad pay dues at their club so they can go there and keep the likes of your mom and dad out." He stares at the shake as if it is the poison capsule he is supposed to bite before he steps onto the mat in two weeks with Chris Byers. *That* is not dues. That is cool, milky, sugary *death*.

"You worry too much," Johnny says back. "Look,

I wasn't going to show you this little trick unless you needed it, but—"

"What trick?"

"Watch." Johnny pulls hard on the straw until his cheeks puff up like a blowfish. He sloshes it around for thirty seconds or more, his facial expressions mimicking one in the throes of the final stages of the most sensual of pleasures, before spitting it into an empty container, then quickly washes his mouth out with water and spits again. He hands the shake to Petey. "It's expensive, given zero nutritional value," he says, "but it works."

"Wrestlers, huh?" the dark-haired girl with the enchanting green eyes says, indicating only minimal interest. "Where do you wrestle?"

"Coho."

"Oh," says her blond, brown-eyed friend, "I know where that is. It's a little Podunk town east of here." She catches herself. "I mean, it's a little place, right? Just a few thousand people." Petey notices Johnny was right. She is a fox, almost as pretty as her dark-haired friend. If he doesn't have to talk, this might not be so bad. He hopes the girls didn't see him and Johnny spitting their milk shake into empty containers. It couldn't have been a pretty sight, nor would it be considered all that intelligent.

"Yeah," he says. "It's pretty small. Good town, though. You ever been there? It's a good town. I guess I said that. Only has a few thousand people. Oh, I guess *you* said that. . . ."

"My friend's mother dropped him on his head when he was born," Johnny says. "Anyway, like I was saying, we're wrestlers. Got a good chance to win regionals this year. Maybe even state."

"That right?" says the dark-haired girl, seemingly taking Petey's measure. "You guys both varsity?"

Petey, hoping to head off any talk of his upcoming match with Chris Byers, breaks in. "Johnny is. He's undefeated since about halfway through our freshman year. Placed at state last year. Probably'll win it this year."

The girls look Johnny over with scarcely more interest than before. "What about you?" the blond asks. "You varsity?"

"Naw. . . ."

"Yeah," Johnny says. "He's varsity. At least some of the time. He's wrestling varsity at one-nineteen in two weeks."

Petey grits his teeth, closing his eyes.

"Really?" the blond says.

"Yeah." Johnny misses Petey's telegraphic pleas,

continuing. "A tough one. Wrestling Chris Byers."

The blond flashes a look of recognition to her friend. "*Really?* I hear she's pretty good."

"She hasn't met up with the likes of Peter Shropshrire," Johnny says. "My friend here gives no quarter on account of sex. Mark my words, he is going to tear her a new one."

Petey's head is about to sink below table level as the blond gazes at him with some concern. "I'll bet that's tough," she says with what seems like genuine regard. "Do the rest of the guys give you as hard a time as your friend?"

Petey grimaces and rolls his eyes.

"But I'm also giving him pointers," Johnny says. "Working him on a double-breasted twisting takedown. If he does it right, he'll end up on the bottom."

Blood floods into Petey's head as the dark-haired girl nearly spits her Coke across the table, choking, then laughing out loud.

Johnny knows his wit has struck pay dirt. As he has always believed, the really classy girls revel in off-color humor. He presses on. "Yeah. I already told him, if she's good, relax and enjoy it. If not, carry her all three rounds. Get the win *and* the goodies."

The girls look at each other and laugh again, shaking

their heads, and Petey begins inching back to an upright position. Maybe Johnny was right. . . .

"Could get his varsity letter on the same night he loses his virginity," Johnny says.

"Yeah," Petey says, getting in the swing, "I—"

The roundhouse right knocks Johnny cleanly onto the cold tile floor, and in a second the dark-haired girl's knee indents his chest. She grips both his cheeks between her fingers and pinches so hard he thinks she's leaving fingerprints. "I think we forgot to introduce ourselves," she says between clenched teeth. "This is my younger sister, Cindy. Cindy Byers. My name is Chris. Very pleased to meet you . . . Johnny, wasn't it?"

Johnny can only nod.

Chris Byers bounces up nearly as quickly as she took him down and turns to Petey. "And you, you little geek. In two weeks I'm going to kick your ass."

"Did you talk about this with your coach?" Granddad asks, pouring himself another cup of hot coffee and dropping to the wooden chair across the table from Petey. He is a large, thick man with a snow white beard and matching hair as thick as the day he turned twenty: Petey's mother's father. He is pushing seventy, which is, as he likes to remind folks, the same age as that actor fella when he started two terms as president of the U.S.A.

"It wouldn't make any difference," Petey says. "He'd just say, 'You volunteered, young buckaroo. Don't wanna go back on your word, do ya?' Then he'd spit a big ol' glob of brown stuff into that cup and proceed to tell me about all the times he volunteered for dangerous missions in Korea. Then all the guys would be pissed at me because it'd be my fault we had to listen to war stories. Most of 'em would rather run stairs than listen to those stupid stories."

"Too bad," Granddad says. "I was in Korea. It deserves better than that." He scratches his thick whiskers and gazes out the kitchen window into the backyard and to the forest beyond. Granddad is the problem solver of the family. Mom and Dad are good for support and for backing you when you step over the line, which seems a common occurrence for Petey, but you just can't beat Granddad for good old common sense. "What kind of friend is this Johnny Rivers anyway?" he says finally. "Way you tell this story, it don't seem like he's helped you out much." He unfastens the bib on his overalls and reaches down inside to scratch.

Petey looks out through the window to those same

woods, where he shot his first and only squirrel when he was fourteen. Granddad taught him to shoot the .22 and even sprang for the license and his first box of ammo. What Petey didn't count on was running over to gather the furry trophy only to discover the triumphant moment turn hideous as he stared into the dead animal's eyes. "Shootin' things ain't for everybody," Granddad said when Petey returned in tears, and helped with a proper burial.

"Johnny's okay," Petey says finally. "He just doesn't know about humiliation. Probably because it's never happened to him." He smiles. "Or he didn't recognize it when it did."

Granddad offers Petey more coffee, which he accepts. It is black and bitter and tastes like a boiled stick; but his stomach has begun to consume its own lining, and it is the nearest thing to food that won't add weight. He needs to drop one more pound before this week's JV match. "You know," Granddad says, pushing his wire-rimmed glasses back up on his nose, "you're the one puts the value on your friendship."

"What do you mean?"

"Just that sometimes a guy like Johnny Rivers needs to know he can't do any old damn thing at your expense."

"Johnny's got lots of friends," Petey says. "He doesn't need me."

"Does he *like* you?"

"I think so. I mean . . ."

"Well, if he likes you, what I said is true. If he don't like you, you're wastin' your time hangin' out with him. But that's for future reference. Seems like right now the problem you got is with this Chris Byers girl."

Petey winces, remembering. "Yeah."

"I got a rule," Granddad says. "When there's a problem, don't do me much good takin' it to anybody but who it's with."

"What do you mean?"

"You got a problem with Chris Byers, take it to Chris Byers."

Granddad easily dodges the spray of coffee Petey chokes on. "What do you think it's like for her?" he continues. "Bein' a wrestler and all, if she's pretty as you say?"

Petey stares again out at the forest. He can't imagine. "I don't know, Granddad."

"That's right. You don't know. An' when you don't know, it's 'cause information's missin'. You think she don't take hard a time bein' a girl wrestler as you do wrestlin' a girl?"

"Yeah, but it's her choice."

"But you don't know why she made it. You want to maybe give yourself a chance to miss out on two weeks of pure anxiety hell, you drive over to Silver Creek and talk to her. And leave Johnny Rivers at home."

In his wildest imaginings Petey Shropshrire can't see himself pulling up in front of Chris Byers's house, placing his finger on the doorbell, and finding the strength to push it.

"Hi," Petey chokes, then grimaces. "Remember me?"

"Not like you're going to remember me," Chris Byers says, standing in cutoff jeans and a loose white sleeveless blouse, one hand on her front door. Her look says she's ready to give it a hard shove and jam Petey Shropshrire's nose an inch or so into his face. "What do you want?"

Petey's mouth opens, but only air escapes, followed by a high-pitched eep.

"Who is it, dear?" A woman's voice from deep inside the house.

"Just a boy," Chris calls back, emphasizing *boy*. She turns again to Petey. "Did you come here just to chirp at me?"

Petey opens his mouth again to speak; but his

tongue and cheeks burn like the driest of hot desert sands, and his throat closes over his larynx like a noose. The door slams, and he's staring into fresh white paint. He breathes deep. It was a fifty-mile drive over broken snow floor conditions.

Well, he tried.

What will he tell Granddad?

He walks to the edge of the porch, ready to retreat down the freshly shoveled steps to his waiting Dodge Dart, then stutter-steps back toward the door. Granddad was right, if he leaves now, he may well die within the next two weeks simply by using up a lifetime of heartbeats. He *has* to try. . . .

He approaches the door; forcing out of his mind how *pretty* she is, he raises his hand to knock. What if her dad is home? What if he comes out? *This guy botherin' you, sweetie? Boy, you better git on down them stairs the way you came.* . . .

Halfway down the walk he remembers it's only four in the afternoon and edges back to the top of the porch. Her dad will be at work. It's now or never. Three times more he stutter-steps toward the door; three times he turns back. Anyone watching surely believes he didn't get his money's worth from his dance lessons. The boogeymen of indecision have blockaded his synapse paths, and finally, in hopeless frustration, he plops helplessly onto the top step, drops his chin in his hands, and waits for his head to clear.

Behind him the door creaks, then from inches behind him: "Jeezus. You are a *mess*. I hope you brought a tent."

Petey doesn't turn. His frustration always brings tears, and if she sees his face, his humiliation will triple. "My granddad told me when I have a problem, I need to face it."

"So turn around and face it."

"I didn't know it would be so hard."

"I guess your granddad never had to carry his cauliflower ear home in a wrestling bag."

"Guess not."

A salty droplet melts a bullet-sized hole in the light skiff of snow on the step below Petey's face. Chris's voice immediately softens. "Jeez, c'mon, what's the matter?"

Petey hates it when the tears come. He can't *talk*. What a wus.

"What are you doing here?" Chris says. "You must have come here for a reason."

"I came to say I was sorry," Petey says, "for the other day. You know, with my bigmouth friend. I was stupid. I thought you guys were laughing, I mean, because you thought he was funny. You'd be surprised how many girls like him. I was just trying to go along with everything. I didn't know you were Chris Byers. I'm not usually like that; I mean, I don't go talkin' dirty to girls or anything like that. Anyway, I was talking to my granddad and—"

Chris places a hand on his knee. "Breathe," she says. "Take it easy. I believe you. I got a little out of hand myself. Everybody's got some smartass thing to say to a girl wrestler."

"Yeah," Petey says, thinking what a genius Granddad is, "I bet. They've got some pretty smartass things to say to anyone who wrestles a girl wrestler, too."

"Guess there are just a lot of smartass folks around, huh?" Chris says.

"Yeah." Petey hesitates then, but decides what the hell, he's on a roll. Who knows how long it'll be before he's talking to a girl this pretty anywhere but in his dreams? "What *did* make you decide to be a wrestler?" he asks. "Not very many girls even watch wrestling. I mean there's mud wrestling and Jell-O wrestling and—"

"Watch yourself."

He bites down on his tongue like it's a hot dog.

"That's not what I meant. I didn't mean you should do that kind of wrestling. I just meant that's the kind you usually see girls doing, I mean if you have cable or go to really bad movies. I didn't mean—"

"Will you stop?" she says. "Boy, you do get cranked up, don't you?"

Petey blushes. Chris Byers isn't the first person who's said that. "Yeah, but why did you get into it? I mean, why wrestling? They have other girls' sports."

"I liked it."

"Yeah, but how would you know that in the first place? I mean, something had to get you to wrestle the first time. You know, like cliff divers. I always wonder how they get themselves to do that the first time." He imagines her discovering headgear in an old Dumpster behind Silver Creek High School when she was six, or looking into the mirror in junior high and thinking earrings would look better in cauliflower ears. Hard to figure.

"Jeez. Does your mind run like that all the time?"

Petey smiles and shrugs. "You mean, like my mouth?" The answer is yes, but he doesn't say it.

"Actually," Chris says, "that's a good question. I have three older brothers. Way older. I was an afterthought, though someone must have told my parents to think again, because there's Cindy, too. . . . Anyway, two of my brothers were state wrestling champs before I was even in grade school, and wrestling was the way they played with me. I learned takedowns before I was in kindergarten. Then in junior high I got into a fight on the playground with this kid named Max Ingalls, who was supposed to be some kind of hotshot wrestler. Took me about fifteen seconds to kick his butt good, just using stuff my brothers taught me, and the coach recruited me to come out for the team. They let me wrestle in junior high, but then they tried to stop me in high school because"—she looks down at her chest and blushes—"because of obvious reasons. At first I agreed with them, but my principal was such a butthead about it—he said if I stayed with it, I could make my parents proud and grow up to be a lesbian, crap like that—and I got stubborn. Next thing I knew, I got my parents to take it to court and there was no backing out."

"Did you want to? Back out, I mean?"

Chris looks back toward the house. "Sometimes. I haven't told anyone that; but I get teased a lot, and it gets real old. All kinds of smartass comments like your friend made the other day, and I got pretty tired of it. If the truth were known, if I wasn't so stubborn and if I hadn't gone all through the court stuff, I'd pack it in.

Sometimes you get yourself so far in there's no way out. That's why I get like I got when you came to the door. But then you cried. . . ."

Petey looks at the ground in embarrassment, partly because he cried and partly because he can't get his mind off Chris Byers's "obvious reasons." All of a sudden the idea of rolling around on a wrestling mat—for lack of better opportunity—with this girl has become not such a bad one. He tries to wipe it out of his head because that's just what Chris is talking about hating, but it does not go easily. He will keep it to himself.

"You know what I like about it?"

"About wrestling?"

"Yeah. I like how you use strength and balance. I love working against muscle—using someone else's strength to my advantage. I like the intelligence. When I wrestled in junior high, I was as strong as anyone I wrestled, but not anymore. I mean, I still need strength, but I have to be smarter to score points."

Petey knows what she's talking about. He has beaten stronger opponents than himself with balance and touch, and other than fielding a red-hot grounder or gunning a runner down at home plate, there is no better feeling in the world of athletics.

"So, I guess part of the reason I've put up with all the bullshit is I like the way it feels. But like I said, I've had about enough. I mean, it's not how I want to be remembered. Anyway, when I get really tired of it, I do what I did to your friend at the mall."

Petey laughs, remembering. "Actually that was about the first time I ever saw Johnny without anything to say. Girls have had pretty bad reactions to his jokes before, but you're the first one to put him on his butt. That was a great takedown. I think it was illegal, though."

She smiles. "I'll use a legal one on you."

"You never know," Petey says. "I'm tougher than I look. Wiry."

"You'd have to be, no offense."

Petey tries to think of a reason to stay; but he's run out of words, and though it's been a pretty mild winter by Montana standards, the chill of night creeps under his jacket. "So, I guess we just do it, huh?"

"I guess so."

He stands. "Look. It was really nice talking to you. I feel a whole lot better than I did driving up here. If I can just keep this conversation in my head, maybe I'll be okay. I'm glad you're not still mad at me."

Chris puts a hand on his shoulder, and Petey notices she's almost as tall as he is. "Me, too. This should be an interesting experience. I've never wrestled somebody I knew before. Or liked."

If the tires on Petey Shropshrire's Dodge Dart touch the road on the drive home, he is not aware of it.

"Is Chris Byers there?"

"Just a moment. Could I tell her who's calling?"

"Peter Shropshrire."

Silence.

"There's nothing I can do about it," Petey says. "It's my name."

"Hello?"

"Chris?"

"Yeah."

"This is Petey Shropshrire. Remember me? We talked on your porch this afternoon. I was—"

"Of course, I remember you. It was only two hours ago. God, you can be strange."

"Yeah," Petey says. "Everybody says that."

"Really."

"Listen, if I came up with an idea that would get me off the hook for wrestling a girl and helped you end your career with a flare, would you do it?"

"I don't know. Tell me—"

"Would you *consider* it?"

"Petey, I don't know. Tell me—"

"Just say you'd consider it."

She sighs. From her little experience with him, she already knows there is no derailing Petey Shropshrire. "Okay, Petey. I'd consider it."

The Coho Wolverines and the Silver Creek Grizzlies line up across the mat from each other in ascending order, lightest to heaviest. In accordance with tradition, each wrestler locks on to the eyes of his opponent directly across the mat and stares him down Mike Tyson style. The orange and yellow of the Wolverines' warm-ups stand in bright contrast to the softer brown on brown of the Grizzlies. Johnny Rivers rocks imperceptibly from heel to toe, beginning his slow ascension to the frenzy that will overtake him moments before he steps onto the mat to devour his challenger. Locked in battle, he is devoid of his loony and often insensitive sense of humor, though the insensitivity remains. There is little question of the outcome of his match tonight, only question of its length.

The result of Petey's match is an equally foregone conclusion, though Petey is the only Wolverine who knows that.

Owing to the unusual nature of Petey's and Chris's

match, an agreement has been reached between the coaches. One-nineteen will wrestle out of turn tonight—wrestle the final match—to equal the import the local media have already heaped upon it.

The two teams seem nearly equal in ability and sport identical win-loss records. It will be very close. The wild card is the Shropshrire-Byers match. Petey is an unknown, having labored most of the year and all of last down on JV. Byers is an unknown talent. She has wrestled two close matches, which she lost by one point, and surprised three other opponents with pins. Is she legitimate? Or did she get a quick drop on her opponents while they were figuring the "gentlemanly" way to take her down? Conventional wisdom indicates the former. Chris Byers has amazing natural strength for a person her size, male or female. Her 12 percent body fat is low even by standards set for youthful, well-trained male athletes, and she can crank out a hundred uninterrupted push-ups as well as fifty chins. She is likely not as quick as Petey Shropshrire, but Coach has warned him consistently he better not let her get ahold of him. Plus what Petey said to Johnny Rivers two weeks ago is true; Chris Byers has to gain on her natural weight to hit 119, Petey has to starve. He could be weak. If all goes as predicted, theirs could be the deciding match.

Al Greer pins his man at 103 for Coho; but Brian Sears's shoulder blades dig into the mat at 1:37 of the first round, and the score is tied. Petey and Chris skip at 119; the rest of the middleweights trade off all the way. Johnny Rivers pins his man at 160 almost before either of them steps out of his warm-up, but by the end of the heavyweight match, Coho is down two points on the strength of fewer pins.

Within seconds of their match Chris and Petey slip away to their respective locker rooms. The buzz of anticipation fills the gymnasium, and opposing chants break out. "Petey! Petey! Petey!" is answered with "Byers! Byers! Byers!" and as the PA announcer calls them to the center of the mat, both explode from the locker room—instantly stunning the crowd to silence. Petey streaks across the gym floor in his bare feet, a thick imitation tiger skin strapped over one shoulder and a four-foot Fred Flintstone Nerf club in one hand. He bellows, "Bigfoot want woman!" as he steps onto the mat.

Opposite him, decked out in a skintight leopard-skin–pattern leotard, Chris Byers slinks across the gym floor. She is Daisy Mae to Petey's primitive Abner. Her long lashes drop, and she turns to the crowd, waving seductively. In the bleachers Petey's grandfather slaps his knee and nods so hard his glasses nearly fall off his nose. The crowd begins to get it, and while the officials and coaches sit stunned, they resume their respective chants. Coach regains his composure first, steps onto the mat, and clamps down on Petey's shoulder. "What the hell are you doing, Shropshrire?"

"Bigfoot bring woman down," Petey growls.

"You get back into that locker and into your gear," Coach says. "I'll try to keep from having to forfeit. Move it."

"Come on, Coach," Petey whispers. "It's just a way to get rid of the tension for all the hype. It's good for both of us. Just let us wrestle."

Coach thinks a moment, glancing across the mat to Silver Creek's coach for guidance. The Silver Creek coach shrugs *why not?* "The foolin' around better be over, boy," he says into Petey's ear. "You win this one or we lose the match. Got it?"

"Got it," Petey says. "Just like the big boys."

Petey drops the club off the edge of the mat and meets Chris Byers at the center, where they lock up hand to elbow in the traditional starting position. The roar from the crowd deafens them, and they barely hear the referee's whistle, but when they do, each appears to work for the advantage. Her mouth close to Petey's ear,

Chris whispers, "One, two, three," and steps back, clutching his forearm with both hands while turning away, and flips him. Petey performs a full airborne somersault, landing flat on his back, roaring like an injured animal. Chris holds her grip on his forearm, stomping the mat fractions of an inch from his head. Petey slaps his palm against the mat in the best Hulk Hogan tradition and bounces on his back as if his head is being kicked. The crowd rises to new decibel heights.

Brent Edwards, the referee, runs the local department store in Coho. His store sports the most complete novelty section anywhere in the state. Brent Edwards loves a good joke. Chris and Petey couldn't have counted on this; both expected to be stopped after their first wild antics, but Brent slides into his role as if he works after midnights on weekends for Turner Broadcasting. With the dramatic flair of a man aced out for the lead villain in his senior class play, he pushes Chris back to the edge of the mat and kneels beside the fallen Petey, lifting, then shaking him. Petey falls back to the mat as if deceased. "I hope you're ready to face Coach," Brent whispers. "I wrestled for him. You'll run bleachers for this."

Petey smiles. "I'm ready."

Brent smiles back. "You're in *love*."

A hand grips the referee's shoulders, and he's pulled back on his butt, as Chris steps back and leaps, executing a perfect knee drop, followed by a patented Gorgeous George Eye Gouge. A guttural roar escapes Petey's lips, and he stumbles to his feet, pawing at his eyes as if that will return his sight, then falls again to his knees, groping toward the edge of the mat where the club lies. Meanwhile, Chris Byers circles the mat, arms extended above her head, welcoming her beloved fans to the world of *real* wrestling. "Men . . . are . . . scum!" She repeats it like a mantra until the female sector of the audience screams it back, stomping the bleachers with each word.

She remains facing her adoring followers as Petey, silently and with great stealth, creeps up behind her with the club.

"Men . . . are—" *Whack!* and Chris Byers stands glassy-eyed a full three seconds before dropping to the mat like a rock.

Petey slings the club over his shoulder, reaches down, and clutches a handful of her hair, dragging her a few feet across the mat. Now the male voices in the crowd erupt.

"Far enough!" Chris says through clenched teeth. "You're pulling it out!"

"It's for the cause," he whispers back, ventriloquist style.

"Far enough," Chris says again, "or the cause will be new teeth for Petey Shropshrire."

Petey stops and drops her head to the mat, standing with one wrestling shoe lightly just below her chest. "Woman . . . kneel!" He starts the chant and is joined by the male population. As their collective voice rises, he steps forward to lead the cheer, and Chris slowly rises behind him. Though his crowd screams their warning, Petey is obviously too wrapped up in their adulation to care. Suddenly he stares into the eyes of Chris Byers, formidable female opponent who was, only two weeks ago, going to make his entire wrestling season a humiliation. She smiles, takes his cheeks in her palms, and executes a World Wrestling Federation text-book head butt. Both wrestlers silently count to three, then fall backward to the mat. Brent Edwards slaps his hand down for the double pin.

Petey Shropshrire is running the bleachers. Bottom to top, down, bottom to top. He started as practice began, and he will finish long after practice ends. His legs will be molten mush. His shenanigans last weekend cost his team the match since Silver Creek led going into it, and no points were awarded for their memorable double pin. Chris and he had agreed before the match that no matter what the score, they would go through with it.

None of that matters. It's Friday. He has run bleachers every night this week, and his punishment will probably end sometime after his thirty-fifth birthday if Coach has his way, which he usually does. He's permanent JV now and won't wrestle another match until Coach thinks he's learned his lesson about letting down teammates, though to his teammates he's a bona fide hero. Chris Byers is no longer a wrestler and therefore has more leisure time. In about an hour or so, even if he needs a wheelchair to reach his Dodge Dart, he's headed to Silver Creek to see a movie with Leopard Lady, the female wrestler of his dreams.

Goin' Fishin'

PREFACE

GOIN' FISHIN'

There is a case to be made that from the time of birth, when we lose a warm, enclosed safe place to be, our lives are made up of a series of losses and that our grace can be measured by how we face those losses and how we replace what is lost. Lionel Serbousek lost his parents in a boating accident when he was fourteen years old. Though he continues to explore his passions—athletics and art—with the fervor of the brash Stotan he is, he remains haunted by his memories of that day on the lake and "what could have been. . . ." Like most of us, when his pain is the greatest, he covers it with anger, anger approaching rage. That rage has the power to consume.

GOIN' FISHIN'

My name is Lionel Serbousek. I'm a high school senior, an artist and a swimmer, and I like to think, finally, a good friend. I'm also an orphan; I live by myself. I can tell no story about my life without telling this one first because it colors everything I do and everything I think.

I woke up on a bright Sunday morning almost three years ago to go fishing over in Lake Coeur d'Alene with my family, and everything was about as great as it could be. I was just short of fifteen—at the top of my age-group—and kicking ass in the hundred fly all over the Northwest. That summer I also sold three oil paintings for money; my father was beginning to respect my talent for the first time. Almost every week my name appeared in the *Spokesman-Review* for being either fast or weird. I won first place in the junior division of the

Spokane Custom Auto Show for my Jeepster even though I wasn't even old enough to drive it at the time. It's a '53 beauty, minus the top, painted fire engine red with an authentic full-scale World War I plastic machine gun mounted in the rear well and Iron Crosses gracing each door. Those who glimpse me in their rearview mirror take immediate evasive action.

I was ready to start my sophomore year swimming with Walker and Nortie and Jeff for Frost High School, where Max Il Song would finally take over as coach. Max had been with us for two years in AAU, and we believed him to be the best coach alive in any sport because he treats you with the same respect no matter who you are, or how fast, and still works you so hard your muscles experience full meltdown every workout. You get *fast* if you swim for Max.

At the beginning of that day things couldn't have been better, but by sundown I felt as alone as if I'd been hatched from an egg by the sun.

I think if human beings had even the slightest capacity to foretell the future, we'd be a completely different animal. *In the moment* that I helplessly watched my family's death unfold before me, I wished I'd lived differently, done my chores on time, told no lies, eaten my vegetables, thanked my parents for giving me a room of my own, told them I loved them, been a better big brother for Kyle.

The person who killed my family was my best friend in fourth grade. He swam backstroke on our medley relay team and stayed over at our house nearly every other weekend; he learned to fish from my dad. His name is Neal Anderson. I still get a card every Christmas from his family, but I have avoided him like AIDS since the day of the accident.

Neal wasn't supposed to be driving his parents' boat that day. They have a summer place on the lake with a private dock and a rocket Sun Runner ski boat, and his parents were in Spokane. Neal and a couple of his buddies got into Mr. Anderson's beer and decided they could take a few spins on the skis before his parents got back. Away from the water it was killer hot that day in late August, and boats dotted the lake like chicken pox.

My father was a head shaker. He was of medium height and build, with jet black hair that was receding toward the back of his head like a grass fire in high winds. He was one of those adults who believe that if you take time to tell your children things, they'll grow up believing them and act accordingly. Anytime that failed to happen, Dad would simply shake his head slowly. With me, Dad shook his head a lot. I was a dreamer who didn't take life seriously enough for his money, and I think that made him afraid for me. More than anything he wanted me to grow up rational. I think he judged himself as a father by the degree to which I could assess any given situation and react appropriately. I never saw much of a temper in him, but I always knew when he was mad at me. "You need to *think*," he'd say. "If you'd just *think*."

Mom would say, "He's an artist, dear. Let him be." You don't get laid back much further than my mom.

If I'd known Dad was going to die, I'd have made a special effort to decrease the number of times a day he felt compelled to shake his head. But I thought I had more time. I thought I had *all* of time.

We set out early, around 4:00 A.M. The lake was about thirty miles from our house on the south side of Spokane, across the Idaho border. We were on the water shortly after 5:00. By 5:30 Kyle had lost his pole when he fell asleep and it dropped overboard. Kyle was five. I was going to let him use mine, but Dad forbade it. He wanted Kyle to know the natural consequences of falling asleep with your fishing pole in your hand.

Fishing was a metaphor for life with my father. It

required all the best elements of what he thought one needed to put together a graceful life. It required patience, knowledge, and skill. It wasn't frivolous, and on a good day you were rewarded immediately for doing it right, though certainly there were no guarantees. Guarantees or no, my dad could catch twenty-inch rainbow trout in an oil spill. You could kid around with him about some things, but fishing wasn't one of them. I learned that at the age of six when we were fishing a slow, lazy river up near the Canadian border. It was my first time out with him, and I had looked forward to it for months. He showed me how to cast my line and watched me do it until I got it right, before moving a few feet along the grassy edge of shoreline to drop his own line in. I glimpsed a fish swimming in a little hole directly in front of my feet, several yards from where my line drifted with the current. In what seemed like a perfectly rational move at the time—and doesn't look *all* that bad today—I quickly reeled in my sinkers and began swinging them at the water as if my pole were a bullwhip, in an attempt to knock Mr. Fish for a loop. After which I intended to reach in and throw his dazed floppy self onto the grass.

Dad had that pole out of my hand on the third swing, and we spent the next half hour discussing the conduct of a True Sportsman. I was not allowed to fish for the rest of that day.

It hurts to remember that the very last time I was with Dad, he was upset with me. Not in a big way, like the time with the socks, when I went to the first day of sixth grade without any—it was in vogue at the time—and they wouldn't let me into school. I simply went back home and painted a pair on my legs—even lettered *Adidas* vertically down the ankles. I really am a pretty good artist, in fact, a *hell* of an artist, and that was one *fine* pair of socks; but they didn't come off as easily as they went on, and Dad was pretty unhappy with me because my age-group swim coach wouldn't let me into the water until all the paint was off.

It took a wire brush.

"You have to *think,*" Dad said, after midnight, on the way to make up the practice I'd missed in the pool at his club. Logical consequences, he said. Dad didn't understand I had to *think* before I pulled boners like that. Plus I couldn't understand why he was upset; they were my legs—my nerve endings.

That day—that last day—he was only *irritated* at me for fishing with poison berries. *Irritated* was a step removed from *truly upset.* I don't even know for sure why I put them on my line; certainly I knew better. We were fishing just offshore, near thick bushes hanging over the water. I was at the rear of the boat, and the worms and salmon eggs were in front with Mom and Kyle, who were fishing together on one pole, unbeknownst to Dad. Mom wasn't all that big on natural consequences when they meant her baby would be bored and whiny all day. I was just too lazy to move to the front of the boat to get the right bait.

"Reel her in," Dad said. "Gonna shoot out to the middle and try for some deep ones."

"I'll leave my line in the water," I said. "Troll a little."

"Reel her in," he said again. "You can't troll at forty miles an hour."

"Go ahead," I said, knowing my dad could spot "what's wrong with this picture" blindfolded with his eyes gouged out, and the second he got a peek at those berries, there'd be a serious discussion, much too serious for six o'clock in the morning.

"*Reel her in,*" he said again, and the argument was over. I tried to get him to start the boat moving while I brought the line in so he'd be distracted, but he waited.

"I have a theory," I said when he spotted my hook near the surface.

"What the hell is that?" he said, ignoring my theory.

"What?"

"On your line. What are you using for bait?"

I grimaced. "Berries."

"Berries. What kind of berries?"

"Whatever was on that bush. Just those orange berries."

"You mean poison berries."

"I don't know that they're poison."

"Would you eat them?"

I stared at the berries trailing my sinker toward us. "I suppose not. Want to hear my theory?"

"I want you to get those berries off that hook."

I took them off and listened to the short version of Dad's "You Got to Do Things Right" lecture for the umpteenth time that summer. I would be going into tenth grade. Things wouldn't be so easy there. Teachers would expect more of me. Childish ways were to be left behind. It was time to *think*. . . .

Dad missed my theory, which was being formulated as we spoke and went something like this: With all those fish in the lake, there have to be some smart ones and some dumb ones. Minnows who listen to their parents and teachers (they travel in schools, remember) and minnows who don't. There have to be some fish in there with shaky upbringings who act just like kids with shaky upbringings. And there have to be a *few,* just a few, whose size is in inverse proportion to their fishy smarts, like Ed Janeczko on Frost High School's football team—six feet five inches, 280 pounds, with an IQ just under his belt size. Now Ed is a pretty rough customer who fights with his mom on a loud and regular basis, and I'm pretty sure if she told him not to eat something, that would be reason enough right there to do it. So, if you follow the theory that all living things are in some ways connected, it isn't too big a jump to figure if I'm patient enough with poison berries on my line, I'm gonna catch the Ed Janeczko of rainbows, and when that happens, I'll surely have the lake record. In effect, I was doing it for Dad.

Neither Mom nor Dad ever got to hear that theory—or anything I've said since.

We were dead still in the middle of the lake in early afternoon, fishing deeper water, when Neal and his buddies, at least two six-packs into the afternoon, decided to take a quick spin in his dad's Sun Runner. Nobody in our boat but me even saw them coming. I hollered; but Mom and Kyle were hauling in a fish, and Dad was shouting advice. They didn't even look up.

And I jumped.

I jumped.

I've watched it over and over, always knowing if I'd stayed a little longer or yelled a little louder, I could have saved them. It runs in slow motion in my dreams, so there's always plenty of time. Of course, in my dreams, no sound comes out of my mouth and my legs are filled with shot puts and they all turn to smile at me.

Neal's boat cut ours in half. None of my family even bobbed to the surface. Kyle's shirt floated near the wreckage, and I dived as deep as I could, only to be surrounded by blackness. The two guys in Neal's boat were thrown clear—the skier cut off to one side—and they screamed and yelled and floundered in the water, trying, I think, to figure out what had happened. I didn't know it was Neal at the time, but I got hold of him and did my very best to drown him. I held him under with both hands on his throat, and it took all the other two had, plus help from a guy who saw it all from a passing boat, to pull me off.

It's funny. There is a feeling in that instant following some life-changing event—at least I think I'm not the only one who has it—that you can step back over that sliver of time and actually stop the awful from happening. But that feeling is a lie because in the tiniest microminisecond after any event occurs, it is as safe in history as the Civil War. Data in the Universal Computer are backed up, as it happens. There is no reverse, not even a neutral. It is that truth that haunted me at first because had I found a way to go back, even if I couldn't have saved them, I'd have stayed in the boat.

Swimming saved me. Swimming and Max. And Elaine Ferral. I have no relatives on either my father's or mother's side, so the state tried to put me in a foster home. They tried eight before they quit. The longest I lasted before hitting the road was twenty-three hours. It was Max who got the Department of Social and Health Services off my back.

"He's fourteen," the caseworker said. "He can't be out on his own."

"He's been on his own since you guys have been in charge," Max said.

"But we can't have it that way."

Max said, "You can't have it any other." When the caseworker started to argue, Max put up his hand. "If you think of his age in years, he's young. If you think of it in *loss,* he's an old man."

She opened her mouth again, and Max said, "And you're making him older. Leave him alone. He's fine. We'll look after him."

I took out my pain on the water. The louder the

whine of the approaching Sun Runner echoed in my head, the clearer the sight of splintering fiberglass and flying bodies, the harder I swam. My teammates, particularly Walker and Jeff and Nortie, pushed hard beside me, as if they could absorb some of my pain, and slowly but surely the searing edge began to dull. I don't know if time heals all wounds, but I know it at least slows the spiritual bleeding.

Elaine. Elaine swam with us in age-group, before deciding greenish blond hair and blood-red chlorine-infected eyes were a definite social stopper. Like any smart, evolutionarily aware, upwardly mobile animal, she opted for dry land sports sometime in junior high. But she was the toughest of us all in her day. In eight years of swimming I never saw her back off once. Out of the water Elaine was the glue that held our group together. She was like a little parent, only smarter, settling minor disputes, helping us hold our course. There's no rational explanation, but some people you just don't mess with, and Elaine Ferral was one of them. And she was there for me always after the accident. She sensed when my loneliness was ready to smother me and would show up with food or friends or just her wonderful self. I never loved her, not like a girlfriend; but I cried with her, and I told her everything.

Elaine Ferral knows my soul, and more than anyone, she walked with me through the land-mined terrain of my grief.

I really thought I had it all in perspective, but then, about a week ago, Neal Anderson showed up at my door. First, I should say my door isn't an easy one to find. My place is best described by my friend Walker Dupree in an essay he wrote last year for junior English:

> I said Lion was an artist at everything he does, but in his personal life-style that holds true only if you're looking for <u>Still Life of Swine</u>. His so-called apartment is two condemned rooms above the Fireside Tavern with a bed, a hot plate, a sink that drains out onto an alley, and—the one really class item—a toilet with a seat belt. He's got a seat belt on his toilet. Claims it keeps him from blasting off. There are no electric lights in this palatial suite, and the sole source of heat is an old electric reflector heater powered by a frayed extension cord running out the window and down to the outlet behind the bar in the Fireside. Artificial light, lest you think these quarters uncivilized, shines from

*a flashlight dangling at the end of a rope
above his bed.*

Mrs. Phelps, our junior English teacher, read that,
gave Walker an A+, and sicced the Department of Social
and Health Services on me again, which brought Max
once again to the rescue. Actually I have enough money
from my parents to live in a much nicer place, but somehow this one fits me like a glove, though Walker calls it
Nouveau Tobacco Road.

Under any circumstances, Neal found me. Through
some miracle of zoning, though we went to the same
grade school and junior high, we don't attend the same
high school. Neal doesn't swim anymore, so I haven't
seen him since the day he killed my family. And that's a
good thing, because when things are at their worst, and
I want someone to blame, Neal's my man. What the hell
was he doing? Why didn't he *think*?

I stared at him through my open door. "What do
you want?"

"Can I come in?"

I barely recognized him, wouldn't have if I hadn't
heard his voice. His dishwater brown hair was stringy and
unkempt, hanging to his shoulders; his clothes were dirty
and threadbare. I considered a moment and said, "No."

He looked away, over the rickety banister surrounding the wooden landing outside my door, then back at me. I couldn't see anything of the happy rich kid I knew in grade school. But it was Neal, it was Neal for sure, and I was instantly aware of my rage.

"Come on, man. I need to talk to you."

"Anderson," I said, "if I let you come in my house, I'll probably hurt you. In fact, I might anyway. You must be out of your goddamn mind. What the hell are you doing here?"

He looked directly at me. "Trying to give myself a chance."

"A chance to what?"

"To make it right."

I gripped the doorjamb, all my resolve directed at stopping myself from pushing him over the banister into the alley. Three years, and his face brought back the rage like a broken dam. "Anderson, turn around. Walk down those stairs. If you see me on the street, cross it. If you see me at a dance, or in a pizza place, or even at a gas station, stop what you're doing and run. I'll let you know if it's ever different."

"Lion, c'mon . . ."

"You must not have heard me."

He started down the rickety stairs, then turned back

about halfway down. I noticed how thin he looked, how raggedy. All his athleticism, that confident gait he had in fourth grade, when he was the sixth-fastest hundred-yard breaststroker in the state, was gone. The Andersons are rich people. They aren't well to do, or comfortably well off, or even upper middle class. They're rich. Their lake cabin cost double what my parents' house cost, and we lived in a nice place. But Neal looked like the poorest of poor kids. I mean, he was dressed bad and all that, but there was more. It was in his eyes. Neal was gone. I forced all those thoughts out of my mind.

I didn't care.

I even wondered briefly about my coldness, but that thought was like a wispy breeze passing through my mind in sleep. It never found space in my consciousness.

He said, "I'm not leaving because I'm afraid you'll hurt me. Nothin' you could do to me would matter. I'm just leavin' because you want me to."

"Whatever reason you use is fine with me," I said. "Long as you leave."

Neal nodded, stood staring a second longer, and slowly moved on down the stairs to the alley.

It was later that night when I realized how vicious I'd been. And it felt good. I have a lot of friends, people who look after me in one way or another and people I look after. Jeff and Nortie and Walker, the guys I swim with, and Elaine—those are people I'd die for, because their friendship is so important. But that night I realized it's my *rage* that's kept me alive over these three years, not friendships. Make no mistake about it, if I had been left alone in the water with Neal that day, I *would* have drowned him. And I have never trusted for a moment since what I might do if I ran into him. Now he was feeling *some* of what I've felt over the past three years, and for all I cared, he could waste away to nothing.

Shortly after the Domino pizza delivery truck left, my phone rang. "Hello. Make it fast, my pizza's getting cold."

"Is this Lionel Serbousek?"

"That it is."

"Lionel, this is Vicki Anderson."

Neal's mom. I closed the lid of the pizza, waiting silently.

"I'll try to make this quick. I know your pizza's getting cold."

"That was just—"

"I know. It was a joke. Listen, Lion, I need to ask you a favor. A big favor. I'm calling about Neal."

I gritted my teeth, waited.

"I know he came and saw you today."

"Yeah."

"Lionel, he's dying."

"Like my parents. My brother."

"Slower," she said. "Lion, I've never known what to say. I'm so embarrassed we haven't contacted you. I couldn't feel worse about what happened. I pray for you every night of my life. Neal's father has set up a trust for you, but we've been afraid to tell you just because we didn't know how to say it. We've just felt *so bad*. I know that's awful—"

"I don't need a trust," I said. "I have everything I need. I'm fine."

"Well, it's there nevertheless. No one can touch it—including us."

"Mrs. Anderson," I said, and felt the heat rising in my chest. "Money isn't going to bring my family back."

"If money could have brought your family back, we'd have already done that," she said. "It's just all we have."

"So what about Neal?" I asked, feeling the cold steel lock again around my heart.

"He needs you to forgive him."

"Won't happen. He killed my family."

I heard Mrs. Anderson choke, then go silent. Then: "Lionel, he hasn't lived with us for more than six months. He's on the street. I think he's using drugs. I can't talk to him. He's dying, Lionel. Please, if not for him, then for me. For his father."

Until that moment I hadn't the slightest inkling of the true power of my hate. The sorrow that rose in my chest for Mrs. Anderson was crushed by it. I said, "Mrs. Anderson, I'm sorry. But do you know what it's been like inside me for the last three years? Do you know how many times I've watched my parents and my little brother get cut in two? Do you know how much I've missed them? Mrs. Anderson, if I thought I could spend fifteen minutes with my little brother starting at the moment of my death, I'd be gone tonight."

Silence again. Then: "I'm sorry, Lionel. I'm sorry I bothered you."

The pizza was ruined. It was still hot enough; but it tasted like hatred, and I ate only part of one piece before splattering it against the wall. I snatched my Speedo and a towel out of the bathroom and headed for the pool at Frost. A couple of years ago the school janitor asked me to regulate the chlorine and pH over one weekend, and I had a key made because I already knew that sometimes swimming is the only way to get what is inside me out before it strangles me.

I flipped the switch for the underwater lights, casting the pool enclosure in that eerie green, and hit the water. I started with twenty-five-yard butterfly sprints, giving myself fifteen seconds between. I have no idea how many I swam, but my chest and triceps were molten steel when I pushed off and saw a body knife into the water beside me. I finished the lap and looked up to see Elaine. I waited the fifteen seconds and pushed off, switching to freestyle. We sprinted twenty-fives at least another half hour without speaking. I thought I could wait her out, but I should have known I could have sprinted all night and she'd still be there. Finally I stopped and hung on the edge at the deep end, gasping for air, still fueled by my wrath.

"Go ahead and leave," I said finally. "I'm okay. I want to be alone."

Elaine said, "Tough shit."

I laid back and pushed off, backstroking a long, slow lap, cooling down, and stood in the shallow end. Elaine was waiting there for me. "I said I was okay," I said. "I just want to be alone."

"And I said, 'Tough shit.'"

I pulled myself out of the water. "Elaine, get out of here. I don't want to talk to anyone."

"Well, you're gonna," she said back, pulling herself out as well, and stood facing me. "I didn't come here to listen to you cry."

"Careful . . ."

She snorted. "What're you gonna do, Lion? Beat me up? Like you did Neal Anderson. Or his mom."

"Hey, don't start," I said, but she took a step forward. Elaine Ferral really is the toughest person I know.

"I'm already started."

"Elaine, we go back a long way, but—"

"It's not a question of how far we go back," she said. "It's a question of if we'll go forward."

"Is that what this comes down to?"

"We'll see."

I walked over to the long table behind the metal rail in front of the bleachers, grabbed my towel, and ran it over my hair and face. "Say what you have to say."

"You treated Neal Anderson like shit today."

"Neal Anderson *is* shit. What happened? That pussy call you up and tell you?"

She jerked the towel out of my hand. "It's for sure no one could tell *you* anything. You're the pussy, Lion. What would your dad say? I knew your dad, Lion, and he'd call game on this cheap bullshit in a second. And your mom—"

Almost involuntarily I lunged forward. "You leave my mom and dad out of this!" I screamed, and my voice reverberated like a handball across the high walls. "I'm warning you, Elaine."

She took another step forward. "Wanna hit me, Lion? Go ahead. That do it for you? Who else do you need to hit? Let's go find Nortie. He's little. And weak. Maybe that's what you need. But let's start right here with me, Lion. Go ahead."

My fist clenched, and my upper lip vibrated like a jackhammer. "I'm warning you . . ." and she punched me in the stomach so hard the wind blasted out of me like a released party balloon. "You double up your fist at me, asshole, you better be ready to use it. You make me sick, Lionel Serbousek. When your family got killed, your friends gathered around you like angels. We spent the last three years making sure nothing touched you, treating you like some kind of boy in a bubble or something. Bad-mouth Lionel Serbousek and you've got his friends in your face so fast you can't breathe."

"You can cancel your friendship out anytime," I said, my breath returning, along with a rush of anguish that must have been down there for three years. "What the hell is the matter with you, Elaine? Neal Anderson killed my family!" I screamed through tears and snot.

"If I ever quit hating him, I—I—I'll die right with them." I dropped to the bleachers like a rock, dazed at what I had just heard myself say.

Elaine didn't budge, but her voice softened slightly. "Lion, remember the night you and Walker and Jeff and I drank all those beers and you took us out on the ice up at the lake in your Jeepster? None of us knew the ice would hold—and it was four miles over icy two-lane roads to get there. You could have killed us. Easy. And anyone else on the road. You were drunk out of your mind. So were we. You could have *killed* us. Me and Walker and Jeff. Your best friends in the world. What if you'd killed us, Lion, and you'd lived?"

"Yeah, well, I didn't. . . ."

"No, but you could have. What you did was no less stupid than what Neal did. Only thing is, the universe caught him and it didn't catch you. That's the *only* difference."

"It didn't happen. . . ."

"But it *could* have. Think about it, Lion. You're an artist. You have an imagination. Think about it."

"It didn't. . . ."

"*Think about it!*" she screamed. "*Think about it, Lion! Think about it!*" She flung the towel in my face and stalked to the bench, sobbing and pulling her jeans on over her wet suit. At the door she turned, wiping her eyes fiercely. "You only get so long to be a shithead, Lion. Just so long to get decent again. Your time's about up."

It was early evening, and I putted along the edge of Riverfront Park in my Jeepster, watching the day people head for their cars as the night people took over. A drug deal here, a grizzly old man packing a raggedy sleeping bag on his back there. Groups huddled by the bridge and over by the bushes along the edge of the YMCA. It was my third night searching.

I knew better than to go into the park at night alone but was way past caring. I'm a big guy—a *tough* guy—and though I know a gang of thugs could take me out, I also know they'd get hurt doing it. Neal's gaunt face had haunted me since Elaine stalked away from me; Mrs. Anderson's pain over the phone had become real. And the thought of losing Elaine lay in my stomach like a sharp rock.

We hadn't spoken since that night at the pool more than a week earlier, and I began to know the power of her friendship through the awful dread of losing it. I could either clean up my act or write Elaine Ferral off. It was the first time since my friends had created my cocoon that I truly understood what could have happened without it.

And yet I couldn't turn off what I felt.

I slammed the door to the Jeepster and walked through the entrance to the park. Suspicious eyes followed me, but I looked into the face of every person I met, hoping to find Neal. I wanted to believe I was doing this because I had come to my senses, but in reality I was learning the price of friendship.

I searched more than an hour and was finally ready to leave and try again tomorrow night—I wouldn't face Elaine again until I found Neal—when I saw a dim light between the slats of the wooden bridge. I walked to the edge and started down, not believing there was a chance. . . .

"Neal?"

He looked up dreamily, eyes glazed. His mom was right about the drugs. The light from his flashlight reflected off the steel bridge beam, casting his face in a gauzy yellow haze. He said, "Who is it?"

"It's me. Lion."

He sat hard on the dirt, dropping his head to his hands, then gazed back to me. His words slurred. "Lion. I killed your mom and dad, man."

"Listen . . ."

"And your little brother."

I said, "Yeah. Look, Neal, I'm not over this yet, but we need to talk."

"No, man, you were right—"

"No, man, *you* were right."

"I was just gonna ski," he said. "I just wanted to ski before my mom and dad—"

"Pack your shit," I said. "I'll get the Jeepster. I was gonna give myself a day off school tomorrow anyway. Maybe you and me oughta go fishin'."

Telephone Man

PREFACE

TELEPHONE MAN

Racism speaks volumes about those who hide behind it, says exactly nothing of those at whom it is directed.

A seventeen-year-old friend of mine, Justin Thomas, understands that truth as most adults in his life don't. Following a summer league basketball game last year, Justin laughingly told his mother the player he'd been guarding called him a "dirty nigger" shortly after he had slapped the third shot into the bleachers. With African, Native American, Norwegian, German—and smatterings of Chinese and French—blood coursing through his veins, Justin could well be the United Nations poster boy.

"What did you do?" his mom asked, a little worried about what he could do at six feet five inches, 235 pounds, and catlike reflexes, but Justin only smiled and

said, "Just what I'd been doing. Get a guy talkin' like that, you can wipe up the court with him."

Racism speaks volumes about those who hide behind it, says exactly nothing of those at whom it is directed.

Telephone Man, from Crazy Horse Electric Game, *is a racist. He's a racist because he has no tools to elevate his status in the world without putting others down, at least in his mind. He has been schooled by a fearful, insecure father to believe he is superior because of nothing more than skin color and place of birth. It is easy to imagine his ignorance was passed to him through generations.*

I have fears in writing a story about racism. In fact, there are a significant number of people who don't understand the simpler truths about bigotry in the same way my friend Justin does and who don't believe that basic lessons are best taught by reflecting the truth. Those people believe when I use the word nigger *or* spic *or* beaner *or any other of a million slurs, I am condoning the use of those words. They think kids should not be exposed in print to what they are exposed in their lives.*

But I believe what I believe, and so I write my stories.

TELEPHONE MAN

If they think I don't know they think I'm weird, *they're* crazier than they think *I* am. I'm not crazy, though, I'm really not. And there's nothin' wrong with my nose, either, except for maybe it gets some pretty big zits on it. People just say that to make me mad. Mostly it's the niggers. They're the ones. Except sometimes it's the white kids, too, and every once in awhile a spic or a Chinaman or one of them Japans, but I bet they get the idea from the niggers. Dad says they're the worst.

Dad says he's sorry he had to send me to another nigger school, but it was the only one he could get me into after I had trouble at my regular school; that's Oakland High, which is a nigger school, too. It wasn't my fault, though. It was because everybody teased me, and then I'd get real mad and do things I don't remember too good, like they said I tried to bash my face through the door to the boys' rest room, and I don't remember that at all. Except they must of been right, I have to admit, because when I started remembering things again, my face was all bloody and my nose was broken. There's nothing wrong with my nose, though, except for maybe a few pimples. Anyway, next thing I knew they were telling my dad to send me to this special school. Only they didn't call it that. They called it OMLC, and it's a lot smaller than Oakland High; but it's still a nigger school. They said I'd get "specialized attention" because there's no more than twelve kids in a class, and that's supposed to be good for kids who are "eccentric"—along with kids who should be in prison. "Eccentric" is what the teachers at Oakland High School call kids they think are crazy. They use words like that so people like me won't know what they're really saying, but I been hearing that word as long as I've been alive because it's what everybody calls my dad. My dad is a fencer—you know, like he teaches people to sword fight—and he's a great guy, even if a lot of people call him Zorro. I don't know why they call him that. He never wears black clothes, and he's not a spic, which the real Zorro was. But he could sure carve a Z in you quick enough. He wouldn't, though, because his name's Carl, so it would probably be a C.

There's a few people I'd like him to carve *something* in, which are mostly the niggers and other colors of people that give me a hard time about my nose—which there's nothing wrong with, I think I already said—or my telephone equipment, which is the most important thing I have. Around this school they call me Telephone Man, which is one of the few things I like, even though I know they think I'm a dork for wearing telephone equipment strapped to my hip. But without it, I feel like how the Duke must feel when they make him check his six-shooter at the saloon door. I feel bare naked. I heard the Duke say that.

I have a deal with André, the guy who runs this place. He's a nigger, but he's not so bad because he makes deals. When I first got here, I went right into his office, real toughlike, because I saw through the outside window on my way in what color he was and I knew you have to shoot first and ask questions later. So I walk straight in there with my dad right behind me, looking good in his white fencer's suit and his mask under his arm, and I walk right up to that André—only I don't know that's his name yet—and I say, "I don't want to go here."

He looks at me and sort of smiles and says, "So why are you here?" and I says, "Because I have to be."

He looks some more and shakes his head real slow and smiles and says, "No, you don't. You don't *have* to be anywhere," and I figure he probably don't know the truth because he ain't white, but already I like the way he's thinking except I can't think of anything to say back, so I turn around and look at my dad.

My dad says, "Good morning, sir, I'm Carl Simpson. This is my son. He's Jack. I apologize for his rudeness." My dad says lots of things about niggers behind their back, but when he's talking right to them, like to their face, he acts like there's nothing wrong with them. He says that's the only way to get by if you're a man of peace like he is. So anyway, my dad just comes right out and tells old André I'm being rude when all I was doing really was getting the jump on him. But André says, "That's quite all right. I like a man who speaks his mind," which confuses me because that sort of puts the nigger on my side and Dad on the other side, and that's not usually how it is, and I'm thinking maybe this André got the jump on *me* while I wasn't looking.

And then, instead of talking to my dad some more about how rude I am, André turns back to me and says,

"So, Jack, if you don't want to be here, why are you here?"

So I tell him, "Because they make you. I'm here because they make you," and André says, "Really? How do they do that?" and I'm thinking this is a *dumb* one if he doesn't already know, but I just tell him what's true, which is they'll put you in jail.

But André shakes his head again and says, "No, they won't, Jack. Who told you that?" I start to say it was my dad, but when I look around at him, he's sort of hanging his head and his face is a little red, and I don't want to get him in trouble even though he's the one that really told me. "My teacher at Oakland," I say, and André says, "Well, your teacher at Oakland was wrong."

So now my head's getting hot and my hair feels all prickly, which is what happens just before I get mad, which I do when I know something's right and somebody tells me it isn't, and I say, "No, *sir*!"

André smiles and starts to put his hand on my shoulder; but I can't stand it when somebody touches me, especially one of *them*, and I jump away. He says, "Take it easy, Jack. What do you think would happen if they put every kid who doesn't go to school in jail?" and I don't get it, so I just stand there feeling my hairs in my head, and André says, "They'd have to build a lot more jails really fast, which would cost a lot of money, and that's the reason you don't go to jail for not going to school," and then real quick he asks me about my telephone stuff. I want to tell him how he's wrong about them not sending me to jail, because it's really my dad who told me that and I know my dad doesn't lie; but I can't do it without getting Dad in trouble, and besides, I don't like to pass up too many chances to tell people about telephones.

"I can fix any telephone that a regular telephone man can fix. I can fix it if the people on the other end can't hear you or if you can't hear them. And if you have more than one phone in your place, I can set them up like walkie-talkies, if they have the right stuff in 'em. See, there's lots of wires inside your phone that you don't get to use because you don't pay for them, but they're there in case you get the money. It wouldn't make much sense if every time you wanted some stupid little thing changed, the telephone company had to bring out all new phones, would it?" and André shakes his head like he thinks I must be right. "So see, it's all in there, but it's dead unless the telephone man wakes it up. That's what I can do."

So André asks me if I want to be a telephone man

when I grow up, and I tell him I'm a telephone man right now, and he says, "Indeed, you are. Maybe I can get you a scholarship, seeing you can fix our phones and probably save us a lot of money."

Well this must not be my dad's day because the next thing he does is ask André if that isn't illegal (my dad says most other colors are experts when it comes to what's illegal, especially niggers), and I think my chances of going here are shot; but André just smiles and says, "I suppose it probably is," but he doesn't say he wouldn't do it, and the next thing I know, my dad is filling out papers and I go to this school. Right before Dad signs the last one, André turns to me and says, "Jack, I want you to know one thing," and I ask him what it is, and he says, "You and I both know nobody can make you do anything if you don't want to bad enough, right? Nobody's making you go here, okay?" and I don't get it, but I say okay anyway because even though it's a nigger school, this is the first place where nobody told me to shut up when I told about telephones.

When I asked Dad later about what André said, he said, "André was wrong, Jack. The law is making you go there. Certain kinds of people don't always pay very much attention to the law."

• • •

Sometimes I wish Hawk wouldn't of saved me from the China kids. I used to call Chinamen chinks because that's the name Dad gave me for them, and it was a good one because they don't like it much. But then I found out my dad must not be as smart as I thought because he told me the Japans were chinks, and so were Vietnams and the people from Korea. But see, I was listening in my history lecture about how a lot of times the Chinamen and the Japans and different ones from all those other countries like that don't always like *each other*. Now I'm pretty sure all of 'em wouldn't go around using the same name for the people they don't like as people call *them* because that just wouldn't make sense. I like to pay attention and get things right, especially when it comes to words, because words are communication and communication is my business because I'm a telephone man, and my dad says whatever you do, you got to know your business. And he ought to know, because he's a pretty good fencer, which is his business.

Anyway, I was telling how sometimes I wish Hawk wouldn't of saved me from the China kids because it confuses me, and I hate that most of all. When a nigger goes saving you from Chinamen, it throws you off because everyone knows niggers are the worst. It all happened on one of those days when I just don't think. That's what my mom and dad both say: "Jack, most of the time you get into trouble because you just don't *think*." I got up late that day, and it looked like I would have to go to school without breakfast again, which happens about every other day. When I do get up in time and wake my mom up, I have biscuits and strawberry jam. A guy needs a good breakfast. Well, Mom was still in bed and the bus was coming in about four minutes and I looked through the cupboards and I couldn't find anything except there was the Bisquick. Well, I knew that's what Mom made biscuits out of, and I figured, hey, even if they don't taste as good not cooked, they have to be just as good for you, right? I mean, your stomach doesn't know if they're cooked. Everything turns about the same temperature pretty quick down there anyway. There wasn't any strawberry jam in the fridge, so I just ate the Bisquick right out of the box, which it was pretty dry. But then, when I was in the bathroom trying to blast off a pimple from my nose that looked about like a spaceship or something, I saw this strawberry stuff sitting on the bathtub, and I didn't know why it was *there*; but I did figure it was no big deal if I ate it *after* the biscuits because like I said before, it all ends up in the same place anyway and your stomach would never know which order you ate it in. Right?

I think it should be against the law to make soap or shampoo that smells like jam and has pictures of strawberries on the front. I mean, it was red and it was thick, and even though it didn't have clumps of strawberries in it and it tasted funny, it looked like syrup, which is close enough to jam to drink when you're in a hurry and just want to get something close to your regular breakfast in you.

Well, what went on inside me probably would of made a good science lesson, I bet. I didn't know how many biscuits you can make out of one box of Bisquick, but I found out later it's a lot. And I also didn't know what happens when you get soap inside you. It's like if you got a lube job.

I was in history when it hit. There was this sort of rumbling inside me, and all of a sudden I knew I had to get to the bathroom really quick, so I just ran for it. I was lucky enough to get my telephone stuff off and up high out of the way, but right after I did that, I started feeling like a balloon that you just let go of the end. I wanted to save my clothes, and I got my shirt off, but my pants got stuck down around my knees right when my butt just turned into a cannon and I was shooting biscuit stuff all over the whole room. It didn't help that I got my clothes almost off. Willie Weaver, the crippled kid that found me—he's the one that cleans up the place after school—said the bathroom looked like a whipped Jell-O factory blew up in there.

I was really scared, even though I never told anybody that. By the time he found me I was curled up in the corner bare naked, because I couldn't tell if I was all shot out or if I was just building up for more rounds, which had already happened twice. I sure didn't want to put my clothes back on till I was all done, and I was also really sick. Anyway, Willie went and got me some clothes out of Lost and Found and snuck me out of the building so nobody would know who did it. When people tease you as much as me, you don't need them knowing you just spray-painted the bathroom out your butt with strawberry shampoo and Bisquick. Willie's a pretty good guy for a crippled kid. Anyway, I was feeling better by the time he got me up, and I begged him not to tell anybody, not even André, and he said okay and that I should take the bus home and change my clothes real quick and if I started feeling bad again, to go to the doctor, but if not, to come back here. He was going to tell everyone my pants ripped and I just went home to change them.

So everything would of been okay except on my way to the bus I ran into the China kids. Now the China kids have been hanging around outside our school for a long time, and if you try to go home alone, they might stop you and take what you've got, like your money or your book bag or your telephone stuff. And I knew they might be out there, but I thought maybe not because it wasn't the end of school, where you might catch somebody going home and take their stuff if you're a China kid, so I took a chance because I didn't want to stay around school and have everybody find out what I did.

Well, there's these steps that you have to go down from our street to the street down below if you want to catch the bus that goes close to my house, and if you don't take that one, you have to walk three blocks farther, and then it takes two transfers to get home if you take that one, and maybe you'll be late if you have a certain time you're supposed to be there or if you're just in a hurry.

The China kids hang out at the top of the stairs, and if they're going to get you, that's where they do it. I saw them there, and right away I was going to go back to the other bus; but our school bell rings outside *and* inside, and I heard it and I knew the kids would be changing classes and some of them would come outside and see me if I tried to go back the other way—and I thought they'd know what I did in the bathroom. I think people just know if you mess up sometimes, even if no one tells them. So anyway, I decided to just go ahead and pretend I didn't see the China kids and maybe they'd just let me go to the bus so I could go change my clothes.

But they didn't. The leader, he's a guy named Kam, was practicing that karate stuff, and the rest of his gang was clapping their hands and saying "way to go." They call theirselves the Jo-Boys. That's a really dumb name, and I don't get it; but I wasn't going to say anything. I just put my head down and walked around the corner to the steps, trying to make it like no one could see me. I can do that sometimes, but not this time. Somebody said, "Hey, kid!" but I just put my head down farther and kept walking. I tried to do it like when you're trying to get past a mean dog. My dad told me not to walk any faster or anything, just to act like I'm not there. But this kid wasn't a dog, and he said, "Hey, kid," again. I tried to walk faster; but somebody grabbed my shoulder, and I turned around toward him and said, "You better leave me alone," but I kept my head down.

He said, "That right?" and I said, "That's right. My dad's a sword fighter, and he can cut your head right off. He'll do it, too, if anybody hurts me."

Then it was a different voice that said, "We're not gonna hurt you," and it sort of tricked me, and I looked up and it was Kam, the leader of the gang, and I didn't quite believe him, but I said, "Okay then, can I just go to the bus?"

But he said, "Well, yeah, but these are our stairs, and we have to charge you to go down 'em," and I said I don't have any money, which was a little bit of a lie because I had enough for lunch, but my dad told me to always say I don't have any.

So Kam says well, how am I gonna get down the stairs, and I tell him, "That's okay, I'll just go to the other bus," because I'm *really* getting scared now, but he says, "Do you see this little area here?" which I think he means where we're standing and I say yes. So he says that part belongs to them, too, just like the stairs and I have to pay to use it. But when I say I won't use it anymore, he just shakes his head and says too bad I already did. Then the kid who talked to me first says, "What's that you got around your waist?" and I tell him it's my telephone stuff. He wants to know what it's worth, and I tell him it's not for sale; but he just laughs, and Kam tells me to take it off.

Now, I'm scared a lot of the time, and most of the time I'm afraid to talk because people just make fun of me because I have this really deep voice and these stupid zits on my nose plus it's hard to get the words in my head out so they sound right. So usually when somebody wants to take something from me, I just give it. But they wouldn't take it, though, if they saw how much it makes me hate them because someday I'll get all the hate together and do something really mean and get even. But anyway, now I'm pretty scared; but they want my telephone stuff, and they're just not going to get it. They're just not. I'm almost nobody anyway, but if I don't have my telephone stuff, I'm *really* nobody. Absolutely, completely, and all the way nobody. So I scream, "Leave me alone!" and they start laughing and kind of pushing me between each other. I grab the buckle to my telephone belt and hold on to it tight, and they push me harder, and they start sort of singing, "Leave me alone, leave me alone, leave me alone," so I scream it at them again, only louder this time, and I keep my eyes closed really tight and hold on to my belt buckle with all my might. Then I hear some girl's voice that sounds like I should know who it is, like she's from our school or something, but I'm not opening my eyes because I don't want things to get worse. Sometimes if I scream and scream and keep my eyes closed tight, things just get over.

But then it starts to hurt. I hear some of the boys telling Kam he could probably kick the belt off me, and he starts to try to do it. By now I'm on the ground, and he's kicking my hands just hard enough to make me let go of the buckle, but I won't, I won't, I never will, and he starts kicking harder and I just lay there and scream.

Then all of a sudden everything stops, and I think maybe it worked, but I keep my eyes closed a little bit longer because sometimes that makes sure everyone goes away. Then I open them just a little and take a peek to see if it's time to get up and run yet.

But what I see is Hawk, and I know I'm done for. See, Hawk is this big nigger that goes to OMLC, and everybody knows if he's after you, you might as well buy a plot in a cemetery somewhere because he might just be the toughest guy in the world. He's never teased me before. In fact, he says hi to me sometimes, but I just figure that's some kind of nigger trick, because that's what my dad said it probably is. Usually Hawk just walks up to me and says something like "Telephone Man, you a kick," and he smiles and shakes his head and walks away.

But now I get it. He gets the China kids to beat me up a little, and then he comes along to finish me off. I think, so that's his nigger trick, and I roll up into a ball because now I know it won't be very long until it's all over.

But then I hear him say, "What you Jo-Boys think you doin' here?" and there's no answer. Then Hawk says, "This here Telephone Man. Friend of mine," and still there's no answer. "How many time I gotta tell you China boys don' go be messin' with my friends?"

My eyes open up now, because this isn't exactly what you expect from a nigger, and I see Kam doing that stuff that Chinamen in the movies do before they start spinning in the air and kicking people's heads in. But Hawk doesn't think that's all such a big deal. He just says, "You done tried that before, Jo-Boy. You 'member that?" and Kam starts breathing big and kind of crouching like an animal; but right before you know it, Hawk's got him down on the ground, and he doesn't get to use any of his karate stuff because Hawk's choking him right to death. The China kid's eyes are so big they're about ready to explode, and Hawk's only using one hand, 'cause he's looking at all these other China guys, who must be thinking they should jump on his back and help out their friend. But nobody does it, they just stand there and Hawk says, "Come on. I be closin' off you number one Jo-Boy air-hole for him; then I take anybody else want some," and still nobody moves.

Then Hawk turns back to Kam and says, "Gonna let you up, China boy. Nice an' slow. You try any you Bruce Lee stuff, gonna embarrass you, front you friends," and he lets a little bit loose.

Kam gets up kind of slow, and when he's about halfway, Hawk grabs him by his cheeks between his fingers and makes him look at me. "You see that boy?" he says. "Got all kinda telephone shit on him?" Kam doesn't say anything, so Hawk moves his head up and down for him, like he's saying yes, and then Hawk says, "You *touch* him, you touchin' me. Unnerstan'?" Kam doesn't say anything again, so Hawk moves his head up and down again. "Now you Jo-Boys, get on. This over here be my school, an' you got no binnis here." Hawk lets Kam go and the Jo-Boys start to leave, and when I look around, I see some of Hawk's friends standing there, waiting to see if they're going to get to fight.

Then the Jo-Boys are gone, and all there is left is his kind and I'm thinking I know niggers are the worst, so maybe they just got rid of the China kids so they could have me all to theirselves to beat up. But then Hawk is helping me up, and this girl named Taronda, who I think I heard her voice before, is looking at my face to see if it's cut and asking me am I okay. It might *still* be a nigger trick; but it sure doesn't feel like it, and Hawk walks me down the stairs to the bus stop and says, "Cripple kid say you got to go home an' change you britches. See you later," and he starts walking back up the stairs. When he gets about halfway back up, he turns and says, "Hey, Telephone Man," and I look up there and he gets a big grin and says, "You a kick. An' you right. Don' be lettin' *no*body get that telephone shit off you. Tha's you one big thing."

So then I'm on the bus and no niggers beat me up like they were supposed to. In fact, they helped me, and so now what was I supposed to do? I quit worrying about it for a while, though, because there was this awful smell, like somebody hung a bunch of strawberries down in the sewer, and I figured out I wasn't all done in that rest room and probably getting beat up made me quit paying attention and I had gone and messed up the sweats Willie Weaver got for me out of Lost and Found. I'm pretty sure the people around me noticed it because of the way they looked at me and then how the ones with perfectly good seats got up to stand near the back of the bus. So I got out at the next stop and walked on home, which took me about an hour when I could of got home in fifteen minutes if I would of stayed on. But while I walked, I got to think a little bit, which is something I don't usually like to do because it makes me feel nervous, and I wondered if my dad would mind if I stopped hating niggers for a while. I really love my dad and I wouldn't stop if he said not to, and I wasn't going to ask him right out because I didn't want to disappoint him—I disappoint him a lot— but I thought maybe if I started giving a few hints about it, that might give me a chance for him and me to talk about it sometime. And I suppose if I had to, I could *say* I still hate them but not do it really, although I know you're supposed to tell your mom and dad the truth.

The guy I'd really like to ask about all this is André, but what if my dad found out I went to a you-know-what instead of him? But if my dad made a mistake about *them*, I wonder if he could of made a mistake about the other colors, too.

In the Time I Get

PREFACE

IN THE TIME I GET

We're all bigots. All of us prejudge people on some basis, be it race, sex, sexual preference, height, age, or any of scores of categories we use to make ourselves seem superior when we are, in fact, feeling inferior.

In the past school year, after his football coach had ordered an illegal hit on a black player from another team, Louie Banks took a righteous stand against racial bigotry and stood his ground heroically as he was stripped of his starting position on the team and generally ridiculed for "not having the stomach" to play Trout football. When all was said and done, Louie was proud of his conduct and eventually saw himself as stronger for resisting the pressure to conform.

But we're all bigots, Louie Banks included. Now, in the summer following his year of Running Loose, another challenge, in the form of his own bigotry, stands before him to be confronted. And the stakes are friendship and basic human dignity.

IN THE TIME I GET

I met him in the Buckhorn Bar two weeks after high school graduation. He was tall and thin, with jet black slick-backed hair and a manner I could now only describe as elegant. I guessed the loggers and cowboys who drank here every weekend wouldn't use that word. At the time neither would I.

I said, "Hi. I'm Louie. Louie Banks. I work here for Dakota. Daytime stuff. You know, replace the kegs, mop up last night's war, run some errands. Who are you?" It was seven-thirty in the morning, and I hadn't expected anyone. Dakota never gets down from his room over the bar until around ten or so when I'm finishing up, so usually I bypass the coin slot and stack up enough country tunes on the ancient Wurlitzer to get through the mop-down and all the dirty glasses.

"Hi," he said back. "I'm Darren. I'm working for my uncle for the summer."

"Dakota your uncle?"

"You people call him Dakota. To me he's Uncle Gene."

"That right? Uncle Gene, huh? I don't think I've ever heard his real name. I didn't know he had any relatives. I mean, I never even pictured him having— Jesus, why don't I just shut up?" I put out my hand, and he clasped it in a brief, firm grip. "Wonder why Dakota didn't tell me you were coming?" I thought out loud.

"He didn't know. I only called a week or so ago, so he didn't have a lot of time to prepare. I haven't seen him for some time, but I visited here often when I was little."

"Where you from?"

"East Coast," he said. "A little town just outside Harrisburg. That's in Pennsylvania."

I smiled. "I just got out of high school," I said. "I know where Harrisburg is. And Baton Rouge, and Pierre, and Providence."

He laughed back. "And Augusta, and Tallahassee. I didn't just get out of high school, but state capitals are about all that sticks with you from those days. That and chemistry valences."

This guy had just summed up my whole school

experience, though my transcript indicates chemistry valences didn't stick. I liked him, though something made me uneasy. "Right. Don't they know if you're ever in any of those cities, you'll see the statehouse and know it's the capital?"

He laughed. Then he said straight out, "You're the guy who lost his girlfriend."

Caught off guard and pretty much speechless, I no longer liked him.

"You don't want to talk about it." He said it as a statement of fact.

"That's not it, exactly," I said, partially recovered. Then: "Yeah, I guess that is it."

"Well, if you want to, *some*time, not necessarily now, I'd like it if you talked about it with me."

I said thanks but didn't really mean it. This guy didn't know me. I barely knew his name. You don't just walk up to somebody and cram a hot branding iron into his tenderest part before you even know if he has a dog or where he's going to college or if he's a vegetarian or something, and I resented that. No wonder Dakota hadn't told me about him; he was probably embarrassed. I snatched a wet rag from the back sink and began wiping off the bar, pretending to ignore Darren sitting on a stool at the end of it. Then I decided to hell with manners and punched up a few country tunes on the Wurlitzer. That should send him hightailing it back where he came from.

Emmy Lou came on first, singing her sweet dreams, with Patsy Cline right behind her, singing exactly the same tune. Old Rob Simes and Nolton Brubaker near to killed each other one night just before closing time, trying to settle who sings the sweetest dreams. Nolton won the fight, so that put Emmy Lou up one, but if you listen close, it's hard to pick. Patsy's got some heart. Plus she gets a few points for singing it first. And probably a few more for dying young.

Anyway, I stuck in some Hank Williams, Jr., and George Jones and Merle Haggard to let him know what kind of a tough corral he'd done rode into and got on back to my work.

"You're angry," he said.

I looked up, faking surprise. "Huh?"

"You're angry. I offended you when I asked about your girl."

"No, I'm not angry," I said. I can be *so* chickenshit sometimes. I swore that I'd quit doing that when Becky died, that I'd be honest no matter what it took, because you never know when you won't have the chance to go back and tell the truth. "I'm just in a hurry to get my stuff done, that's all. I'm not mad."

"Then why are you punishing me with that?" he said, nodding toward the jukebox. "It was an offense, but it wasn't a felony."

I smiled and dropped my rag on the bar. "Okay," I said. "I'm a little sensitive, I guess. A lot. Nobody I knew ever died before. And I didn't handle it so great if you want to know the truth. I mean, I trashed her funeral, yelled a lot of bad things about God, really messed up some people's heads. . . ." In my mind I saw my best friend and my worst enemy, a hand under each arm, helping me out of the church through the stunned silence of the congregation. That's how crazy it was.

Darren put up a hand. "You don't have to explain anything to me. I just wanted you to know I knew about her so you wouldn't be careful around me. We're going to be working together and all. I know a little bit about death."

I let his last sentence pass, wondering why Dakota had told him. Is that how people refer to me now? *That guy? Oh, that's Louie Banks. His girlfriend died. . . .*

Darren asked me to show him around, so I reached around the back of the Wurlitzer and kicked the volume down a couple pegs, then gave him the grand tour—which lasts maybe ten minutes—through the back storage coolers and into the narrow opening off the end of the bar where Dakota keeps all the beer nuts and pickled things, like eggs and pigs' feet and jalapeño peppers. If it don't go down easy, pickle it.

He told me he was twenty-five years old and that he went to college at Penn State for two years before deciding to take a break and travel around the country for a while, till he could decide what he wanted to do in the world and quit wasting his tuition on Early Tibetan Philosophies and Creative Uses for Nuclear Waste, which I don't think is really a class but made the point. I told him I was almost eighteen and headed for a little college up in eastern Washington called Clark State, where I had a partial scholarship to run cross-country. He said since he dropped out of the university, his parents weren't exactly ecstatic about the way he was living his life and had written him out of his inheritance, which was one reason he came clear across the country to see Dakota. Dakota was never real close to his parents anyway, Darren said, even though Darren's dad was Dakota's half brother. He said the inheritance was worth probably more than a million dollars, but it didn't mean much anymore. I said it was hard to imagine a million dollars not meaning much, that I could be written out of my parents' will and never know the difference, given what they had to put in it, but that they stood by me in the very worst of times. I said I didn't know if that was better than a million dollars, but it had to be the next best thing.

He said it was the *best* thing. Then he told me about his death sentence. Darren had AIDS.

What I did is I panicked. I did my all-time sloppiest cleaning job and left before I found out any of the things I would want to know later: like did Dakota know, and how long did he have, and how could I get him to stay away from me if he was going to die because that was just what had happened to me already. Darren must have seen how messed up I was, because he backed way off and didn't say anything more except to ask me not to tell anybody. I said okay, because how could I say no, but God, I *knew* I'd end up telling *some*body, because AIDS isn't something you just get, like flu. How you get it is the thing. I instantly knew why I'd felt uneasy before; his *elegance* was something I normally associated with someone who's a homo.

So who do you talk to about *that*? Nobody I knew. I did know I wanted to get as far from him as I could. I'd had about all the death I needed for a while, and *everybody* knows you stay as far away from faggots as you can.

So I lay in my bed that night, long after midnight, twisting and turning so much the sheets almost mummified me, repulsed by what I thought about Darren, and maybe a little ashamed because I thought it, because this voice in me kept saying, "Hey, this guy is *dying,* and no matter what else is going on, still, he's dying," and I knew a little bit about how final that is. Those mixed-up thoughts got me thinking too much about Becky, which created so much anxiety I knew I wouldn't get one bit more sleep, and the only thing to do was get up and run.

My family doesn't get alarmed anymore—or try to stop me—when I run in the middle of the night, though my little sister calls me Night Speed and asks in front of my friends whether I wear a cape. Night runs have been my common practice since the funeral, and they think it's what I do to keep my head on straight, which is correct.

The moon was nearly full, and I watched my faded shadow skim over the pocked blacktop stretching the three miles toward the river bridge where Becky crashed that day. I've never told anybody this—people think I'm crazy enough as it is—but I still talk to her sometimes. The reason I loved her so much—besides that she was heartbreak pretty—was that she made sense in ways most adults in my life don't. She was less cautious—ready to take risks—and she always saw things from a simpler perspective. Plus she stood up for herself, which is the hardest thing for me. Christ, after Coach Lednecky ordered a killer hit on Kevin Washington to put him out of the Salmon River game because he was afraid one player—one black player—would wreck our perfect season, it must have taken me fifty attempts to quit. I wanted to be on the football team so bad I kept forgetting what I believed in. Quit. Want back. Quit. Want back. You'd have thought someone nailed one of my feet to the ground and whipped me with a quirt. But Becky stood right up and said what she thought, and that helped me finally stick to it, and it's the main reason I still talk to her; because I can listen to her voice and then steal her words for myself and sometimes it works because her words have so much integrity.

So have me committed. I hear voices.

What I said to Becky, and I'm not proud of it, was this: "So what if this guy's a faggot? So what do I do then?"

I think it's good to ask a dead person about someone

who's going to die. Becky didn't answer. That should have meant something.

After the night of my midnight run I avoided Darren like he had AIDS. I hated knowing his awful secret, and I resented the hell out of him for telling me—like I was supposed to *do* something about it. I began cleaning the Buckhorn at odd hours when I was pretty sure he wouldn't be there, or I'd take Carter with me so Darren wouldn't have a chance to talk. He never pushed, but sometimes I'd see him looking at me in a way that made me do a major-league squirm. God, I wanted him to go back where he came from. For one thing, what does it mean when some homo likes you? Just ask anyone.

"So what do ya think of my nephew?" Dakota came down early that day, caught me sneaking around cleaning at 6:00 A.M. He couldn't have had more than three and a half hours' sleep.

"He's okay," I said. "Haven't seen him around too much. He work till closing?"

Dakota nodded, hoisting himself up on the bar. The bar's got holes all over in it from him doing that. One of his hands is a hook. "Yeah. He says you're keepin' clear of him."

I looked away, stacking dirty glasses from a tray beneath the bar, while my face burned and my heart hammered. I can't lie to Dakota. When Becky died, he saw me naked.

Dakota came in the side door of the Buckhorn. We were two hours past my having completely trashed Becky's funeral, screaming at the big-city preacher who didn't even know her, cursing God Himself before the horrified eyes and ears of the congregation. Dakota would have been well within the confines of decent human behavior to kick my butt across the bar and back. But he looked to my pain. "Figured that must be you," he said. "Want some company?"

I nodded. "Yeah, I guess I do."

He stood there in the doorway and just looked at me. Finally he said, "Louie, it ain't safe."

"You're right," I said, "it isn't. I gotta tell you, Dakota, I don't get it. Man, what did Becky ever do to get killed? What did any of us ever do? It just ain't right."

"Nope," he said. "It ain't right, that's for sure."

For only the second time since she died, I burst into tears. My chest heaved, and snot ran from my nose in ropes. "It's just not fair," I said. "Where's God,

Dakota? Where is He?"

"Louie," he said, "I ain't educated much; but I listen pretty good and I see pretty good, and one thing I'm sure of is that if there's a God, that ain't His job. He ain't up there to load the dice one way or the other." He paused, thinking, and his voice went soft. "Boy, if you come through this, you'll be a man. There's one thing that separates a man from a boy the way I see it, and it ain't age. It's seein' how life works so you don't get surprised all the time and kicked in the butt. It's knowin' the rules."

"The rules," I said. "How can you know the damn rules? They keep changing."

"Naw, they don't," he said. "It's just that you have to learn the new ones as you go. That's the hard part. Learnin' the new rules when they show theirselves. You go on blamin' God, you get no place. You got to understand that the reason some things happen is just because they happen. That ain't a good reason, but that's it. You put enough cars and trucks and motorcycles on the road, and some of 'em gonna run into each other. Not certain ones neither. Just the ones that do. This life ain't partial, boy."

As I started out the door, he stopped me. "Louie."

"Yeah?"

"If you was walkin' in the middle of the road an' you saw a big ol' truck comin' right at ya, you wouldn't stop an' ask the Lord to get you out of the way, would ya?"

"No," I said. "I'd probably just get off the road."

"Well then, don't be goin' askin' Him to get ya out of the way of all the other crap that's comin' at ya." He held up his hook and looked at it. *"You go on an' take care of it yourself."*

Dakota lives in my soul. To my credit, I didn't try to lie to him about Darren. "Yeah, I guess I am keeping clear of him. You know why?"

"Tell me."

"Do you know about him, Dakota?"

"Tell me."

"He's sick."

"Bet he told you not to tell me that."

"He did, but—"

"Did you tell him you'd keep quiet?"

"Yeah, but— Dakota, I don't know what to do."

"Well, if you said you'd keep quiet, you should keep quiet."

"But—"

He nodded slowly, scratching the end of his nose

with the hook. Someday he's going to slip. "It's a test, Louie. He asked ya not to tell. Ain't many places that boy is safe. You must know that."

"So you know?"

His eyes said yes, but he didn't nod or speak.

"Can you tell me how—"

Dakota shook his head. "Nope. I said I'd keep quiet."

Frustration clogged my throat. One of the worst things ever would be losing Dakota. "Dakota, I don't know what to *do*!"

"Ain't much precedent for it," he said. "Leastways not around here. Guess you do what you want."

"But—"

"Louie. Anything you wanna know you got to ask him. I got no better ideas than you 'cept to tell the truth."

"Jesus, why me?"

"Same reason your girlfriend died," he said.

Just because. An accident of time and space.

I entered the back door of the Buckhorn at 8:00 A.M., back on my normal schedule, and punched up some Waylon and Willie, turning the volume up so Darren couldn't help but know I was alone. He'd already heard Carter tell me he'd take wire snips to the cord if I played that shit in *his* presence. My palms sweated so bad the broom kept slipping from my grasp, but I danced it across the floor behind broken glass and chicken bones and peanut shells and pickled pepper stems like it was just another normal day.

"Hey, friend, how've you been?" He stood in the doorway to the stairs leading up to his room.

I looked up. "Okay. How 'bout you?"

"Some up, some down, I guess," he said. "This disease doesn't give you much warning." He looked to the Wurlitzer and smiled. "Your heroes really always been cowboys?"

"Not always," I said, wondering what Roy Rogers would think of me being alone in a semidark bar with a man of questionable sexual preference. "For a while there some of them were fighter pilots." I paused a minute, staring at my broom, then said, "Look man, I'm sorry. You told me you have AIDS and I ran away. I should have stayed and at least talked about it."

He said, "It was a pretty normal response. I'm dying. And I'm dying in an ugly way. Not many people want to have anything to do with that."

I said, "Yeah, well, that ain't all. It would help to know . . ."

"How I got it?"

I took a deep breath. "How you got it."

His eyes leveled on mine. "I'm gay. I got it having anal intercourse with another gay man who was infected."

Dakota would call that a "sludge hammer to the chest." I'd promised myself to be cool, but I hadn't expected anything about anal. I know I stood there looking about as stupid as is possible for a human being to look, and I know it was only shock that kept me from hightailing it again.

He said, "I don't have time for anything but the truth, Louie. Would you rather I were an intravenous drug user?"

I hated to admit it, but *yes*.

"Can't help you," he said. "I've always taken good care of my body. Didn't want any bad stuff in it." He shook his head and smiled. "Nice try, huh?"

I leaned the broom against the bar. By now Waylon and Willie were headed for Luckenbock, Texas, and I wished I were with them.

He smiled again, but his lip quivered. "I'm pretty scared, Louie."

"Why'd you come here?"

He hesitated. "I'd like to talk about this with you, I really would. But this is a small town, and my uncle would lose this place in a flash if anyone knew about me—about the AIDS. I wasn't going to tell anyone but Uncle Gene, but after he told me how special you were—everything you'd gone through—and I met you, well, I had to try. There's something about you. . . . Your girlfriend died, and I thought that gave us—I thought it made you like me in some way, you know, closer to death. I was involved in a support network back in Pennsylvania, and that helped a lot; but things got so bad with my folks I just couldn't stay. It was as if I got sick just to shame them. I couldn't stand them looking at me like I was—like I was so *dirty*." He took a breath, began to go on, but stopped. "I have to know you're not going to tell anyone. If you are, give me a week, and I'll get out of here. I have to know. People around me have just been in too much pain—"

"I won't tell," I said, and I knew this time I wouldn't.

Then Darren told me what it was like to have AIDS, to wake up every morning wondering whether this would be the day you'd start sliding for the last time into that pitch-black pit that sucks all your energy dry and leaves you with nothing but open sores your body has no power to heal, or to walk around in a world knowing if the people on the street could look one millimeter under your skin and see your disease—or just your pain and fear—they'd whirl away in disgust. And he told me about keeping hope going, how sometimes he could do it merely by feeling an evening breeze brush his face or putting his feet in the cool water up at the lake or watching Dakota tend bar as if he had three hands instead of one. "Any little thing that seems magic," he said. "That'll do it sometimes. I've never been so scared, Louie, but I've never soared like this either."

But the worst thing he told me, at least the worst in my book, is that no one ever *touched* him anymore. No one who knew—who cared about him—ran his fingers through Darren's hair or patted him on the back or shook his hand. "Most people know you can't get it that way," he said, "but it's far too ugly for them to take a chance." He was quiet a moment, looking into my eyes, and I got nervous. "Don't worry," he said. "I won't ask you to touch me. I know why people don't do that. I know about fear."

There's something about you. . . . I wished I could have just listened to his story, but what was the *something*? Something that made gay people like me? I took health class. I knew about latent homosexuality and all that. God, you try to be nice to somebody. . . . The last thing I needed to think about was *something* about me.

• • •

"Look at this," Darren said, carefully removing a long blanket from the top shelf in his closet. I stood next to the window in his tiny room above the Buckhorn, as far from him as I could get and still be in the room. I mean, what would happen when people finally figured out he was gay and then somebody found out I'd been in his room?

He unrolled the blanket to reveal what appeared to be an immaculately cared-for deer rifle. The hardwood stock was oiled and finished with such care the grain actually seemed to have depth, and the light through the tiny window facing Main Street glinted off the dark blue steel of the barrel like a laser point.

I said, "*That* is a good-looking gun."

"Would you like to go try her out?" he asked. "I haven't had it out of the closet since I got here."

I looked away.

"Oh, hey," he said. "I understand. You have your friends. You've been spending too much time with me. . . . Louie, are you afraid I'm going to make a move on you?"

"What? No, of course not," I lied.

"You are, aren't you?"

"*No.* I mean, maybe I thought—"

He shook his head. "Jesus, Louie, I have AIDS. If I had sexual relations with anyone, it could *kill* them. I would never do that."

I stared at him, silently, and felt foolish.

"Besides," he said, smiling, "you're ugly. Give me some credit for taste."

"Actually," I said, "that's only part of it." I looked again to the rifle. It was beautiful. "See, I'm not much one for guns. I was born in the wrong part of the country. I just can't shoot things. I tried it once, but there was this chipmunk—" I laughed. "I just don't have the stomach for it, that's all. Coach said that was what I was missing in football."

"Then you'll love this," he said. "Here." And he handed it carefully to me. "Look down the scope."

I did, aiming out the window, above the buildings across the street, and out onto the North Fork of the Payette. A flock of greenheads skied to a stop on the glassy expanse of the river, more than a mile away. They appeared to be landing on the end of the barrel. I said, "Jesus, that's a powerful scope. Where'd you get that?"

"Pull the trigger," he said.

I looked up at him, then back down the scope. "No, thanks. My daddy told me don't play with guns."

"Go ahead," he said, "pull it."

I looked up again, and the crazy idea jumped into my mind that he might be grooming me to shoot him. Like when the time came and he couldn't stand it any-more. Jesus, being around this guy just kept offering up more and more shitty possibilities.

He smiled. "I'm not messing with you, Louie. Go ahead, pull the trigger. You won't hurt anything."

I squeezed. Click! whrrrrr.

"Pull it again," he said.

Click! whrrrrrr.

"Isn't that great?" he said. His smile ran ear to ear. "It's a *camera*."

I lowered the rifle from my cheek and examined it carefully, then brought it again to my shoulder and pulled the trigger. "You're getting a lot of pictures of the top of that building," Darren said, pointing to the Chief Café across the street.

I said, "Jesus Christ, it *is* a camera. Why—"

"Because there are parts of Pennsylvania where hunting is as big as it is here. I got tired of people using the fact I don't like to kill things to prove I was a faggot. So I cut my losses. Cost me a bundle, but it was worth it. It would have cost far less, but I had to buy a pickup so I could mount a gun rack. Then I bought a red and black plaid jacket and a baseball cap that said, 'God,

Guns, and Guts Made America Great' and by golly, I was one of the guys." He looked over the rifle with pride. "And I'm getting to be a pretty darn good wildlife photographer, too." He looked down. "At least I was. Let's go. If you like it, maybe I'll leave it to you."

"No, I couldn't—"

Darren put up his hand and smiled. "Don't hurt my feelings, man. I'm dying, remember?"

I crouched forward, leaning into my wide receiver's stance as Carter Sampson stood beside me with the ball, taking a make-believe snap. "Hut one, hut two, hut three . . ." and I drove down five steps, hard, and cut across the middle. The ball touched my fingertips, and I cut again instantly upfield. "Nice one," I said. "You're gonna be too good to believe, Cart. The U. doesn't know what a deal they got." I flipped the ball back to him.

I loved working out with Carter. We had spent all of last summer—the summer before our senior year—running laps and wind sprints, lifting weights, and running countless pass patterns. It was to be my year, two years of bench time about to pay off. By the end of the summer Carter knew my every move, could float the ball into my hands with his eyes closed. And he was my best friend, the kind of friend who could and would have taken me right to the top with him.

Then, in the second game of the year, Coach Lednecky ordered a chickenshit hit on Salmon River's black big-city-transfer superstar, and I got moral. So much for Louie Banks's run at the N.F.L.

But when it was all said and done, and I looked back, the games were never it anyway. It was those summer workouts with Carter. Out on the field under the hot summer sun in my shorts and cleats with my best friend, who *was* a bona fide superstar, running pass routes and dropping for push-ups and sit-ups and planning our lives. That's what it was really all about for me. Later, when I became accustomed to my role as Louie Banks, the Guy Without the Stomach for It, I looked back, and the best part was still there. And here we were again, getting Cart ready for the U. I think I'll do just fine in the world never being great if I can just *touch* greatness once in a while.

"Sideline," Carter said. "All the marbles." He crouched into the position, "Hut one . . . hut two . . . hut three . . ." and I angled for the sideline, meeting it about ten yards out, then sprinting for the goal line. Carter dropped back—danced a little for show—patiently waiting for me to cover the distance, and unloaded. The ball dropped perfectly into my outstretched fingertips as I crossed the goal line. What a magical arm on that guy.

"Where you been the past couple of weeks?" he asked as I flipped him the ball.

"Right here. Remember me? Louie Banks, slowest wide receiver to ever stop a Carter Sampson bullet with his bare hands?"

"I meant nights."

"Just around, I guess." I felt embarrassed. "Been hanging out with Dakota's nephew some. Till he goes to work. Why? You been getting off early? Wanna do something?"

"Naw, I'm still working late. I just heard you been hanging out with that guy."

"Darren?"

"You just better be careful, buddy."

"Careful of what?" When in doubt, play stupid.

"Banks, I don't know whether you've figured it out or not, but Dakota's nephew is a faggot."

"What? You really think so?" It's hard for me to lie to Carter; he's my best friend, but I promised. At least he didn't know the other part. Yet.

"Come on, Louie. Look at the way he moves. Look at the way he talks. You ever see him with anyone? A girl, I mean?"

"Sampson, this is Trout, Idaho. I haven't seen you with a girl all summer either, but that doesn't mean you're a faggot. It just means there aren't many girls here. The guy's twenty-five years old. Who's he going to go out with?"

Carter looked away, like he always does when he thinks I'm being a dumbshit. "Okay, Banks. Just remember I warned you, all right?"

"All right." I was disappointed, having thought I could get through all this without losing anything. But what did I expect? Up until just a few weeks ago, when I walked the backwoods with Darren and his trusty 30.06 deer camera, learning to look at life for the last time, sucking in everything around him that smelled of mystery—and sharing it with me—a homosexual was just about the worst thing a guy could be. Homo. Switch hitter. Queer. Queen. Faggot. And some so bad I won't say them.

But he was just Darren. When I didn't have to worry about what anyone else was thinking, he was just a funny, sad guy with a chest bulging with the kind of courage I hoped to have someday. In the face of death he could hold steady and take a perfect shot. He never made anything that felt like a pass at me, and he liked animals. And God, he was going to die.

I wondered what it must be like to be called those names when you're going to die. It would be bad enough if you were going to live. Maybe those names could make you *want* to die. Who knows? I sure didn't want to get into it with my best friend, though, and what I thought was this: If I keep spending time with him, I could lose Carter. I've seen that look in his eye before, and it's not one you argue with. Then Darren would be dead and my friend would be gone. Boy, nothin' comes cheap.

I ran patterns for another half hour or so, until I was really bushed; but we didn't talk much, and I could feel a thin wall going up between us, which scared me more than anything. I think when somebody important in your life dies, you get afraid to lose anyone else, and Carter was one of the few people who stuck with me through all the craziness of my last year, when I must have looked like the biggest bozo this side of Ringling Brothers. I was *so* afraid of losing him, hating to think of myself without someone as fine as Carter Sampson—or Becky Sanders—in my corner. One down . . .

I tried desperately the rest of that afternoon to catch every pass, as if that would help maintain our connection, because the look in Carter's eye had been hard when he said that word *faggot,* and I knew Darren's sexual preference wasn't a point Carter was willing to compromise on. I didn't understand yet that Darren's sexual preference required no compromise, that it was none of Carter Sampson's business. But in one way I was no better because I hadn't accepted it either. I just blocked it out, didn't think about it.

Carter plopped on the grass next to the steel frame of the blocking sled and dug into his workout bag, drew out a large bottle of Gatorade, offered it to me.

I took a long swig and handed it back. "Look," I said, "you might be right about Darren. I don't know. But he's okay. I mean, he's not trying anything with me, and he's kind of lonely, okay?"

Carter looked at me that way he does, without speaking, and took a long drink.

"Cart . . ."

"Better stay away from him, buddy."

"Maybe you're right," I said, and at that moment believed I would simply avoid Darren for the rest of the summer. No way I could afford to lose Carter, and besides, if Carter thought he was gay, then so did a lot of other guys, and I didn't need everyone thinking that about me. Not along with everything else.

"I am right," he said back. "You're my friend. I don't give my friends bad advice." He stood to walk to his car.

AIDS didn't tarry. On the afternoon of July 19, two days after my birthday, I came home from my second job—pumping gas at Norm's service station—to find a message on Mom's answering machine: "Hey. Louie. Haven't seen you for a while. Look, I'm up in the county hospital for a while. Why don't you come up and see me if you get a chance?" There was no mistaking Darren's voice. I mean, in one sense Carter was right: He did sound like what you think of as gay. Stereotype or not, that's what he sounded like.

God, I didn't want to go. My commitment to Carter aside, the remembrance of death was so fresh I could almost smell it, plus I'd seen enough news stories on TV and pictures in the paper to know some of the bad things AIDS usually does before it lets you go, and I was really afraid to see that up close. But *because* of last winter, I knew there isn't any time to hesitate or be squeamish about death. It comes when it wants, and whether you're the one going or the one staying, you better have your shit in order, or you're going to wind up hating yourself for all you wish you'd done. A day hasn't gone by that I didn't wish I'd said one more thing to Becky, or touched her one more time, or told her who she was to me.

I should have parked around back, out of sight of the main road, but I pulled up directly in front of the main entrance. The rooms are small, and Darren was back by himself all the way at the end of the hall behind the front desk. There were probably only three or four other patients in the whole place. I remember wondering if they put him back there in case anyone in town figured out why he was in there, so nobody would have to go by his room.

The worst part is nobody touches you.

"Hey, man," I said at the doorway, "how you doin'?"

"Been better," he said.

I stood there, nodding my head.

He said, "Come on in. I'm no more contagious than I ever was."

"What happened?"

"Sometimes it just comes after you," he said. "Any little old germ just has its way. You have nothing to fight back with."

I knew Darren couldn't have lost much weight in such a short time, but he looked like he'd dropped about fifteen pounds, most of it around his eyes. I walked on into the room and sat in a metal chair beside his bed.

"Guess I don't look so hot, huh?"

I shook my head. "Not so hot."

He said, "Tell me about Becky."

"What do you want to know?"

"I want to know what it's like to be left behind, what happens to the people who don't die. I'm worried about the people I love."

No time for anything but the truth. "Well, it hurts," I said. "A lot. You get angry that you didn't do every little thing just right when the person was alive, and you get angry at the person for dying. It's crazy, I know, but you do. And sometimes you hate everybody in the world who isn't feeling as much pain as you are, and as much as anything you hate God, if you can still believe in Him, for not stepping up and fixing things."

Darren looked up at the ceiling, and there were tears in the corners of his eyes. "That's not how I want it to be," he said.

I remembered Dakota's words to me and said, "Well, Darren, that's the way it is."

He was quiet a minute. Then he looked over at me and took a deep breath. He said, "Louie, would you hold my hand?"

To this day, I hate myself for what I almost said. I almost said no. And it wasn't because I was afraid I'd get AIDS. It was the other reason. But I love myself for what I did say. I said yes. I said yes, and I reached over and put his hand between both of mine. It was real awkward, and I know he probably felt that; but I did it. And I'm glad because now I don't have to look back and wish.

It's funny. It's almost as if we weren't in Trout anymore. Nothing inside that room was like anything else in my life. As I sat with his fingers sandwiched in mine, I thought again about what it must be to go through the last part of your life without being touched. Especially if it happened when you were only twenty-five. Becky and I had touched each other all the time. I don't know how I could live now if we hadn't.

I told Darren about all the good memories I had of Becky and how I'd get together with her dad once in awhile and just talk about her—how we kept the good things about her alive by mentioning them, how people who die can actually stay alive through the people who cared about them and learned things from them. I told him I still talked to her. And I promised I would talk about him, too.

Then I looked up and saw Carter standing in the

doorway. He said, "I saw your car. . . ."

Instinctively I jerked my hands free from Darren's, but it was too late. Carter grimaced and shook his head, then walked away. Darren opened his eyes in time to see Carter's back, and I think he sank a little. If there's one thing I could change about all that happened, it would be that moment.

I saw Darren one more time before they transferred him to the hospital in Boise, though he didn't see me. I went for a visit; but Dakota was there, and I didn't want to interrupt, so I stood in the doorway. Dakota was up on the bed with him, his grizzled old arms around Darren's shoulders, and he was kind of petting Darren's head with his good hand.

". . . really scared, Uncle Gene. *Really* scared."

"You'd be damn fool not to be."

"I wish I could clear things up with Mom and Dad."

"Some things are just too hard," Dakota said. "Your daddy just don't have the heart for it. He's gonna be real sorry, boy, an' I'll sure tell him what you wanted for him."

"He just couldn't understand about me being gay. I tried to tell him—"

"I don't understand it neither," Dakota said, "but it

ain't the point. The point is you're blood. An' you're sick. An' you're a good boy. Somebody oughta rap your daddy one alongside his head, but I don't reckon it'd do much good."

"You'll tell him, though."

"I'll tell him."

Darren shifted a bit to get more comfortable, his eyes still closed. "About Louie . . ."

Dakota looked up at me in the doorway. He'd known I was there all along. "Louie'll be fine," he said. "That's not a boy you need to worry about."

Darren relaxed. "See that he gets the camera, okay?"

"Done."

"Tell him if he gets tired of talking to Becky, he can talk to me."

Confusion passed briefly over Dakota's face, but he said, "I'll tell him."

"Uncle Gene, I wish I understood this. I only learned I was gay a couple of years ago, and then, before I even got to deal with that, I was sick, and now I'm almost gone. I've been a Christian all my life and a pretty good person, I think. I haven't stolen, or lied more than the next guy, or cheated anyone out of much. There are all these things I was supposed to learn, and

• • •

"Long time," I said, stepping from the pickup. I reached into the bag in the back and pulled out a football, flipping it to Carter.

"Yeah," he said.

"You quit throwing for a while?"

He looked right at me. "Nope. Been throwin' to Mark Robeson some. A little to Boomer."

"Boomer. You must really be pissed at me."

"I told you that Darren guy was a fag," he said.

"I already knew it."

Carter shook his head. "Now we all find out he had AIDS. I suppose you knew that, too."

"Yup."

"Man, Banks, I don't get you. I thought we were supposed to be friends."

"We are supposed to be friends," I said.

"So what kind of a guy hangs out with a homo with AIDS and doesn't tell his friends? AIDS is serious shit, man. When it's around, everybody should know it. What if somebody caught it somehow?"

I started to answer. I started to say I wasn't doing anything that could give me AIDS and neither was Carter so he didn't have to worry. I started to say how being careful is one thing, but being crazy is another—

and to tell Carter what it was like to look a dying man in the eye, how much bigger my heart was. But I didn't. I didn't say any of those things because I was getting ready to lose him. "Look, Cart, I don't have AIDS, okay? Let's just throw some balls."

He was steamed, and the first four or five passes came so hard they almost went through me, but I held on to every one, jogging back and flipping him the ball as if he'd just floated another feather onto my fingertips. We didn't talk anymore, and that was the last time we worked out before leaving for our respective colleges.

I think I passed Carter up that day. All my life I've wanted to be like him, be able to throw a football fifty yards through a tire or pop a twenty-five-foot jumper or drive through the streets of Trout leaning back in my bucket seat with an elbow out the window, people on the sidewalk truly believing I owned the town. But that day *I* was bigger. That was the day, knowing all I had to lose, I quietly turned and stood my ground.

I'm in college now. I made the cross-country team. I'm not the best they've got, not the worst. But I'm going to do what I heard Dakota tell my dead friend Darren. I'm going to see how far I can go in the time I get.